DANGER IS EVERYWHERE

A HANDBOOK FOR AVOIDING DANGER

by DR. NOEL ZONE
"THE GREATEST DANGEROLOGIST IN THE WORLD, EVER"

with the help of my neighbors
DAVID O'DOHERTY (words)
and CHRIS JUDGE (pictures)

Little, Brown and Company
New York Boston

Text copyright © 2014 by David O'Doherty
Illustrations copyright © 2014 by Chris Judge
Cover art and design copyright © 2014 by Chris Judge
Text in excerpt from *Danger Is Totally Everywhere* copyright © 2016 by David O'Doherty
Illustrations in excerpt from *Danger Is Totally Everywhere* copyright © 2016 by Chris Judge
Text and illustrations in excerpt from *Draw-It-Yourself Adventures: Alien Attack*
copyright © 2016 by Andrew Judge and Chris Judge

Little, Brown and Company
Hachette Book Group
1290 Avenue of the Americas, New York, NY 10104
Visit us at lb-kids.com

Originally published in 2014 by Puffin Books in Great Britain
Published in hardcover and ebook by Little, Brown and Company in October 2014
First U.S. Trade Paperback Edition: April 2017

Little, Brown and Company is a division of Hachette Book Group Inc. The Little, Brown name and logo are trademarks of Hachette Book Group Inc.

The publisher is not responsible for websites (or their content) that are not owned by the publisher.

Book design by Chris Judge

Library of Congress Control Number: 2014946052

ISBNs: 978-0-316-50183-5 (pbk.), 978-0-316-29929-9 (ebook)

Printed in the United States of America

LSC-C

10 9 8 7 6 5 4 3 2 1

This book is dedicated to my next-door neighbor Gretel.
I hope she finds out someday.

—Dr. Noel Zone

Many thanks to everyone who gave me feedback
while I was working on this book.

"I tore out the pages and used them to clean my mountain bike. Now please get out of my shop and never come back."
—Alfie Donohoe, local bicycle-shop owner

"We couldn't burn your book in the stove in the zookeepers' hut because a giraffe had already peed on it."
—Roxanne Cantwell, zookeeper

"I put it under the leg of my desk to stop it wobbling. That is the only good thing I can say about your book or handbook or whatever it is."
—Saskia Hill-Candles, librarian

"How dare you suggest that any of my teachers are vampires!"
—Mr. Staples, school principal (POSSIBLY A VAMPIRE)

"FURRY FACE! HELMET HEAD!"
—some local children

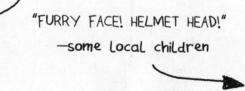

I haven't heard anything from Gretel yet.

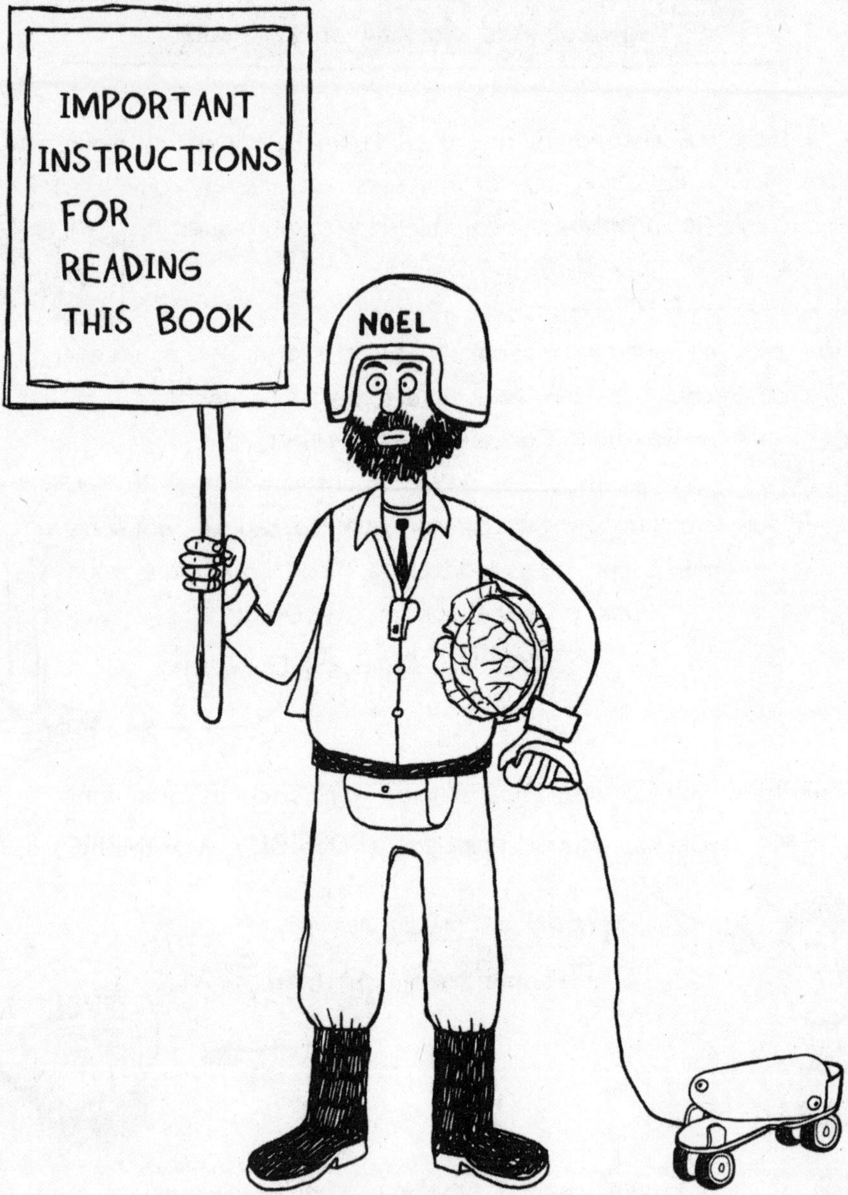
IMPORTANT INSTRUCTIONS FOR READING THIS BOOK
NOEL

INSTRUCTION 1

Make sure you are reading it in **A SAFE PLACE**.

EXAMPLES OF SAFE PLACES TO READ THIS BOOK

---

1. In bed, having checked underneath the bed for **A SLEEPING TIGER**.

> **NOTE:** If you have a pet cat, **MAKE SURE IT ISN'T A TIGER**.

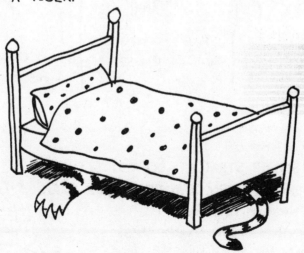

We will deal with how to check if your pet cat is a tiger **LATER**.

2. Leaning against a tree.

NOTE: MAKE SURE IT IS A TREE AND NOT
A HUGE VENUS FLY TRAP OR OTHER HUMAN-EATING PLANT.

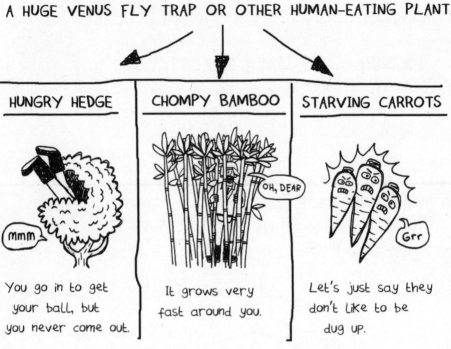

HUNGRY HEDGE

mmm

You go in to get
your ball, but
you never come out.

CHOMPY BAMBOO

OH, DEAR

It grows very
fast around you.

STARVING CARROTS

Grr

Let's just say they
don't like to be
dug up.

3. Sitting in a chair.

WARNING: SIT UP STRAIGHT! DO NOT SLOUCH!
SLOUCHING IS VERY BAD FOR YOUR BACK.

In the long run, slouching is just
as bad as these other things.
Note: Also make sure that your
chair is **NOT** on fire.

EXAMPLES OF UNSAFE PLACES TO READ THIS BOOK

1. On a bicycle, while being chased by wasps. Or just **ON A BICYCLE. (I HATE BICYCLES!)**

2. In a shark cage, while dressed as a sandwich. **(SHARKS LOVE SANDWICHES.)**

3. In a chair that is on fire.

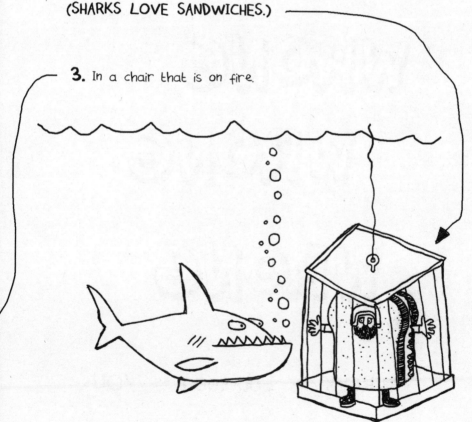

INSTRUCTION 2

CHECK FOR SCORPIONS.

You probably think that reading books is a safe thing to do.
Nobody has ever been injured while reading a book, you probably think.

WRONG
WRONG
WRONG

WRONG × 1,000,000 = YOU

If you think you're safe, then you have never heard of

THE PAGE 9 SCORPION,

an awful, horrible bug that likes to wait on page 9 of books,
and when you open that page

IT LEAPS ONTO YOUR NOSE AND ATTACHES ITSELF THERE.

So, from that moment on, you have to
explain to everyone you meet that you didn't know about

THE PAGE 9 SCORPION,

and that's why it's there, in the middle of your face,
firing poison from its bottom.

HOW TO CHECK FOR THE PAGE 9 SCORPION

1. Close this book slowly and put it
   on the ground.

2. Now jump up and down on the book
   a few times, like it is a small,
   disappointing trampoline.

3. If you hear a crunching or crushing sound,
   **CONGRATULATIONS. YOU HAVE
   SAVED YOUR NOSE.**

Now continue to **INSTRUCTION 3.**

5

INSTRUCTION 3

DO NOT READ THIS BOOK TOO FAST!

This book is full of fascinating information.
You may find it so incredibly interesting that you whiz
from page to page, faster than any book you
have ever read before.

BEWARE!

If you read it too fast, outside, on a hot day
with the sun shining down,

THE WHOLE BOOK COULD BURST INTO FLAMES.

So it is a good idea to have a fire extinguisher
or bucket of water beside you, in case you smell
burning or see smoke rising from the pages.

NOW YOU MAY READ THIS BOOK.

THANK YOU.

I CAN'T BELIEVE
YOU FORGOT
ABOUT THE
PAGE 9 SCORPION
ALREADY.

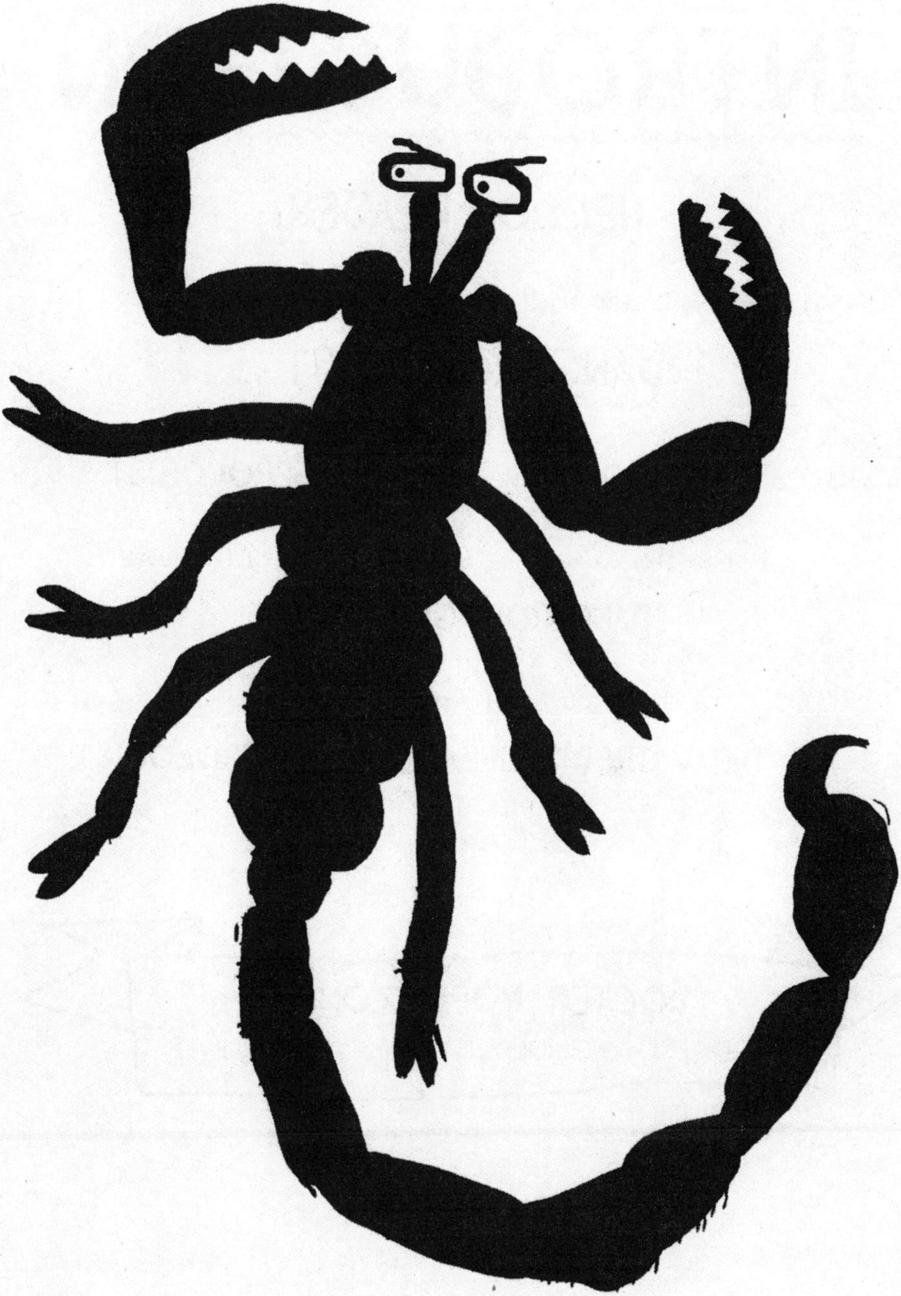

INTRODUCTION

HELLO, READER.

My name is Docter Noel Zone and I am a

DANGEROLOGIST.

In fact I am **THE WORLD'S ONLY DANGEROLOGIST.**

I know this to be true because I invented the word

DANGEROLOGIST.

So you could say

I AM THE WORLD'S GREATEST DANGEROLOGIST.

Or even:

DOCTER NOEL ZONE:
THE GREATEST DANGEROLOGIST IN THE WORLD, EVER

Thank you.

Note also that I am **DOCTER**, not **DOCTOR**.
A doctor has to spend years just learning to be a doctor.

I gave myself the first name **DOCTER** so I could concentrate

all my energy on being a **DANGEROLOGIST**.

It saved a lot of time and hardly anyone notices the spelling.

WHAT IS A DANGEROLOGIST?

A **DANGEROLOGIST** is a person who is
an expert in **DANGEROLOGY**.

WHAT IS DANGEROLOGY?
DANGEROLOGY is the area of expertise of a **DANGEROLOGIST**.

PLEASE EXPLAIN WHAT A DANGEROLOGIST IS, WITHOUT USING THE WORD "DANGEROLOGY."
Oh, OK. While you probably see the world as an exciting place
where you can go on adventures and ride your bike,

a **DANGEROLOGIST** sees it as an awful place
where terrible things can happen, **ALL OF THE TIME.**

ARE YOU AGAINST FUN?

No! No, no, no, no, no! **I AM NOT AGAINST FUN.** Not at all.
But the problem with fun is it makes you forget that

DANGER ~IS~ EVERYWHERE

EXAMPLE: You probably like climbing trees.
That is a fun thing to do, you think.

WELL, TELL ME IF THIS IS FUN:

1.

You climb a tree, but when you are halfway up you come across

A GIANT EAGLE SITTING THERE.

2.

And you go to climb down, but it picks you up in its beak and takes you to its

SECRET EAGLE CAVE

in a forest.

3.

There it makes you sit on its
GIANT EAGLE EGG FOR MONTHS,
occasionally feeding you worms
FROM THE GROUND,
which you have to eat because
THERE IS NO OTHER FOOD.

4.

And then when the baby giant
eagle finally hatches it thinks
you are its mother and hugs
you for another week.

5.

Until eventually it flies away
and leaves you there in a
cave, very far from
anywhere and past where
the regular buses go.

6.

So it takes ages to get home
and **IS ALSO VERY
EXPENSIVE**
(train + bus fare).

DOES CLIMBING TREES STILL SOUND LIKE FUN?
ANSWER = NO

HOW DID YOU BECOME A DANGEROLOGIST?

An excellent question. I used to work as a

SWIMMING-POOL LIFEGUARD.

The pool had all the usual safety restrictions:

- No diving
- No running
- No dunking
- No cannon balls
- No sneaky peeing
- No lovey-dovey kissing

But soon I began to see lots of other dangers that people weren't being warned about:

WALKING around the side of the swimming pool is dangerous.

GETTING INTO THE WATER is dangerous.

SWIMMING ITSELF IS VERY DANGEROUS.

SO I BANNED ALL OF THESE THINGS.

In fact, I banned moving of any kind.

But then there was a new problem. If people don't move while they are in water, they sink to the bottom,

WHICH IS EVEN MORE DANGEROUS.

And then I had to rescue them with my long stick with a hoop on the end that looks like a huge version of the thing you blow bubbles through. For a while, I was a very busy lifeguard, blowing my whistle until people stopped moving, and then saving them with the giant bubble thing.

And then I realized the real problem with swimming pools:

WATER!

Water makes everything wet and slippery. It can get in your mouth and up your nose and into your ears. It can make you very tired from swimming in it.

Water makes everything **DANGEROUS.**

The answer was simple:

I GOT RID OF

ALL THE WATER.

I emptied the pool completely. You could still get into it, but you had to carefully climb down a ladder and lie on the cold tiles at the bottom of the empty pool in your swimsuit and hat.

DEEP END

Soon nobody came to my swimming pool anymore, and it had to close down. **AND I WAS DELIGHTED!** I had managed to make a dangerous place

NOT DANGEROUS AT ALL.

Thank you.

16

WHAT IS THE POINT OF THIS BOOK?

That is another very good question. **GOOD QUESTIONING!**

There are **TWO MAIN POINTS** to this book:

1. To remind you that

DANGER
IS
EVERYWHERE

2. To make **YOU** a qualified **DANGEROLOGIST** (Level 1)

ME? A DANGEROLOGIST! HOW?

If you manage to get all the way to the end of this book and it hasn't **BURST INTO FLAMES** or you haven't been **ATTACKED BY ANYTHING** and the whole thing hasn't **TERRIFIED YOU TOO MUCH,** then you can take the **DETBAFOD** on page 232 (Dangerology Examination To Become A Full-On Dangerologist).

If you get all ten questions right, you will be allowed to sign the **DOD** on page 241 (Diploma Of Dangerology (Level 1)).

That means that you, too, can call yourself a **DANGEROLOGIST** (Level 1) and make your own

Tɪɴʏ Cᴀᴘᴇ Oғ Dᴀɴɢᴇʀᴏʟᴏɢʏ

(T-COD)

and put the word **DOCTER** before your name.

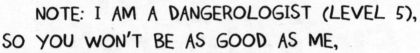

NOTE: I AM A DANGEROLOGIST (LEVEL 5), SO YOU WON'T BE AS GOOD AS ME,

but, still, it's a start.

And together we can show the world that

DANGER ⚡IS⚡ EVERYWHERE

Thank you.

Docter Noel Zone

THE GREATEST DANGEROLOGIST IN THE WORLD, EVER

(neighbor of Gretel)

UNBELIEVABLY IMPORTANT!

UNBELIEVABLY IMPORTANT!

★ SPLOD ★

(Special Protocol Language Of Dangerology)

As a **POD** (Pupil Of Dangerology) you will need to get used to the **SPLOD** (Special Protocol Language Of Dangerology).

The **LOAD** (Life Of A Dangerologist) can be very busy:

★ **LOFDing** (Looking Out For Danger),

★ **POWDMBing** (Pointing Out Where Danger Might Be),

and

★ **MSTDIDWEEIPSTIAing** (Making Sure There Definitely Isn't Danger Where Everyone Else Is Pretty Sure There Isn't Any).

Often there isn't time to use full words.

EXAMPLE: You're having a picnic with your friends in a quiet corner of the countryside, when suddenly a **CHEETAH** appears out of the forest.

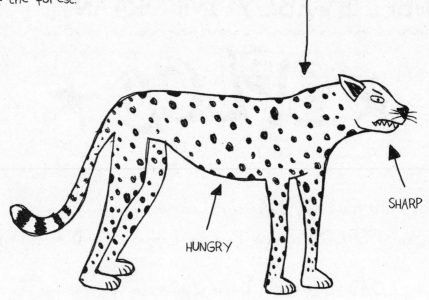

HUNGRY

SHARP

A **PWINAPOD** (**P**erson **W**ho **I**s **N**ot **A** **P**upil **O**f **D**angerology) would probably say:

"OH NO! IS THAT A CHEETAH COMING OUT OF THE FOREST? WHAT AN UNEXPECTED THING. DOES IT WANT TO EAT OUR SANDWICHES? NO, WAIT. IT WANTS TO EAT . . . AAAAAGH . . . AAAAAGH AAAAAGH!"

And in that time I don't need to tell you what has happened.

(CLUE: run, run, run, chomp, chomp, chomp.)

But a **POD** or **FOD** (**F**ull-**O**n **D**angerologist)
who sees this happen will know to shout:

"TIACA!" (you say it like **"tee-a-kaaa"**)
which is short for: **"This Is A Cheetah Alert!"**

Then any other **PODS** and **FODS** who are present will know to
stand up and **START DANCING**.

Cheetahs, along with all big cats and grumpy people
at weddings, **ARE TERRIFIED OF DANCING**. It scares them
more than somebody who is not a **POD/FOD** seeing a cheetah.

The animal will immediately turn around and run at high speed,
back into the forest.

As you will see, this book contains a great deal of **SPLOD.**

Here is a quick guide to the basics:

AAAAaAAA

A very important one, short for:

(Advice About Avoiding Angry and Aggressive Animal Attacks).
You say it like you are going AAAAaAAA, but with a quiet bit
in the middle for the "a."

This book contains plenty of **AAAAaAAA**
along with some

TTTFADIES

(Top Ten Tips For Avoiding Danger In Everyday Situations).
So if you are going on vacation, for example, you should check
the vacation **TTTFADIES** along with the **AAAAaAAAs**
for any dangerous animals that may be found where you're going.
Vacations should be enjoyed. But they should be planned

WAFOS

(With A Focus On Safety).

DAD

In **DANGEROLOGY**, your **DAD** is not your father but your **D**anger **A**lerting **D**evice.

This is a whistle, worn around your neck, that signals to other **DANGEROLOGISTS** that there is **DANGER** nearby.

WARNING!

Never toot your **DAD** at a soccer game. The players will all stop playing, and everyone will be very unhappy with you.

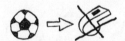

BEWARE!

Do not get a **DAD** with a toot that is too high-pitched. It could act as a signal to dogs in the area, making a dangerous situation even more dangerous.

CAUTION!

Your **DAD** is not your **DOD**, which is your **D**iploma **O**f **D**angerology, the award you will get if you complete the **DETBAFOD**.

★ FASPLOD ★

(**F**urther **A**dvanced **S**pecial **P**rotocol **L**anguage **O**f **D**angerology)

NAAD

(**N**ot **A**t **A**ll **D**elicious)

A warning that something should not be eaten.

RED

(**R**eally **E**xtremely **D**elicious)

The opposite of **NAAD**.

For example: "That cake is **NAAD**, but this cabbage is **RED**."

NOTE: This does not mean that the cabbage is a red cabbage.

It means that it is **R**eally **E**xtremely **D**elicious.

To make sure people know you mean **RED**, say it a bit louder than you would say "red."

NOTE 2: Cabbages really are **RED**. They are my favorite food, and also an example of an **ANDAAO**

(**A**bsolutely-**N**ot-**D**angerous-**A**t-**A**ll **O**bject).

PEBB

(Personal Emergency Bum Bag)

Every **DANGEROLOGIST** needs a **PEBB** around

their waist, full of important **ADEGs**

(Anti-Danger Equipment/Gadgets).

T-COD

(Tiny Cape Of Dangerology)

It's like a name tag for

DANGEROLOGISTS.

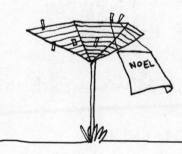

TID

(That's Incredibly Dangerous!) Something **DANGEROLOGISTS** say a lot.

NED

The opposite of **TID** is **NED** (Not Especially Dangerous).

Between them is **GABMD** (Getting A Bit More Dangerous). Very occasionally, you will encounter something so dangerous that **TID** is **NOT ENOUGH.**

The **SPLOD** we hold back for these rare occasions is:

RAD

which is **R**eally **A**wfully. **D**angerous.

If your day looks like it might have anything **RAD**,

maybe you should **SIB** (**S**tay **I**n **B**ed).

TEPOC

(The Emergency Page Of Calm)

While the aim of this book is to **TEACH** you that

⚡ DANGER IS EVERYWHERE ⚡

Parts of it may also **TERRIFY** you so much that your hands shake and you can't bring yourself to turn another page.

This will seriously affect your chances of completing the **DETBAFOD** to receive your **DOD**.

If at any point it gets **TOO SCARY,**

I have included this page, **TEPOC.**

This is the most relaxing and calming page I can think of.

Feel free to return to this page **AT ANY POINT** and stare at the picture until you feel OK to continue.

If you are still scared after five minutes of staring,

you should probably lie down and maybe **SIB** for the rest of the day.

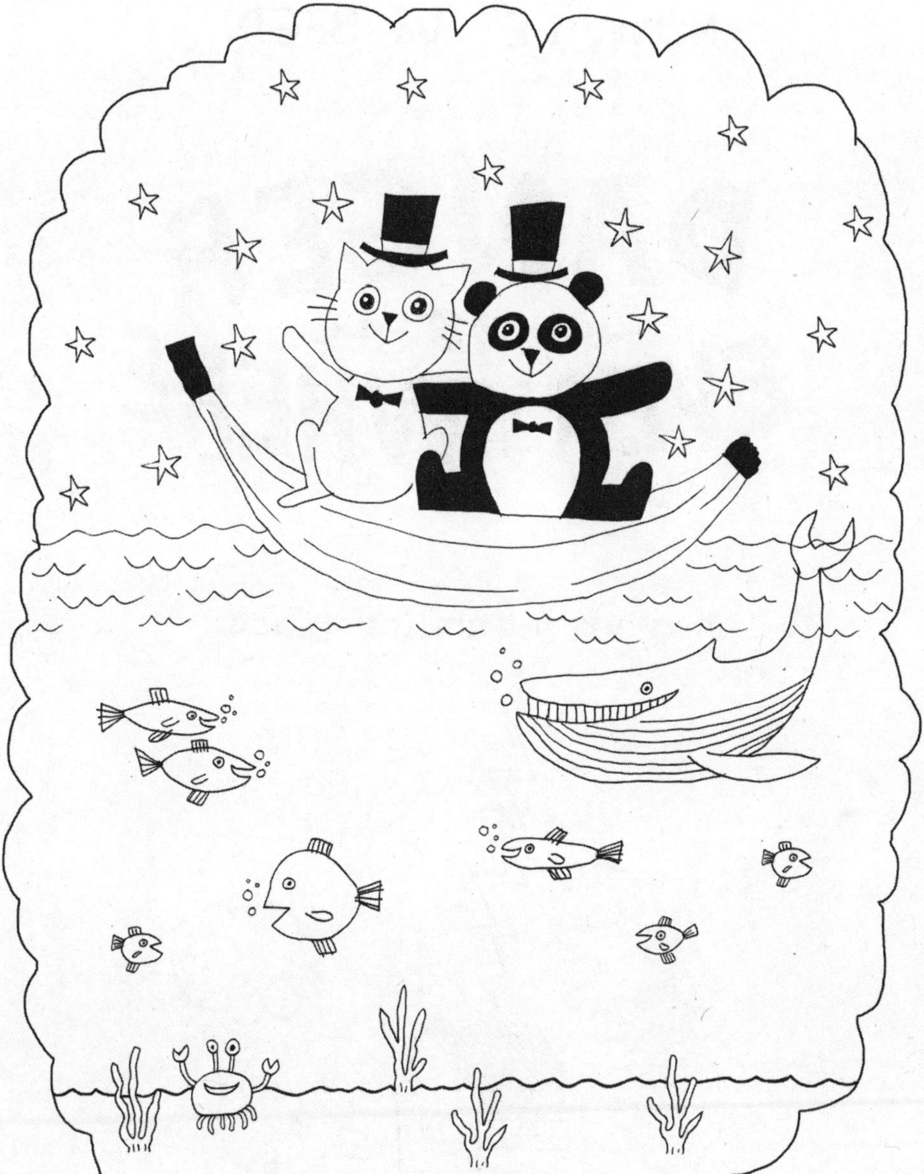

NOW, LET US BEGIN

DANGER IS EVERYWHERE

in a very familiar place.

DANGER IN THE BATHROOM

Your bathroom seems so safe. All that toilet paper and the soft towels and bubble bath. Nothing dangerous at all there, you probably think.

OH MY GOODNESS, I CAN'T BELIEVE HOW WRONG YOU ARE.

The bathroom is the second-most dangerous room in the house for people who have **A RHINO ROOM** (a room with an actual rhino living in it—**RAD**), and it is the most dangerous room for everybody else.

And what makes the bathroom **ESPECIALLY DANGEROUS** is how you often visit it **WHEN YOU ARE SLEEPY.**

ZZZ...

NOEL

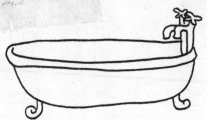

31

First thing in the morning and last thing at night are two of
the most dangerous times of day. Along with:

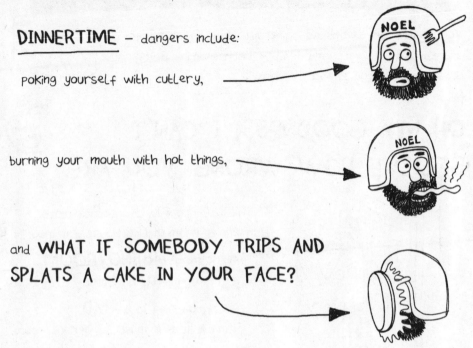

DINNERTIME – dangers include:

poking yourself with cutlery,

burning your mouth with hot things,

and **WHAT IF SOMEBODY TRIPS AND
SPLATS A CAKE IN YOUR FACE?**

THE AFTERNOON – dangers include:

Meteorite

going outside,   staying inside,   and everything else.

THE EVENING – dangers include:

board-game accidents
(for example, getting a dice stuck up your nose),

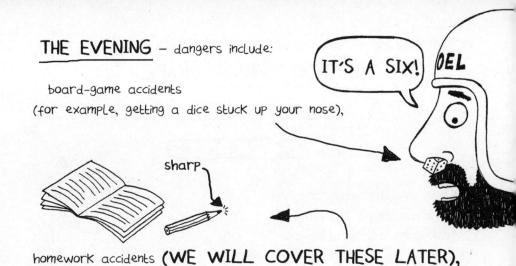

homework accidents **(WE WILL COVER THESE LATER),**

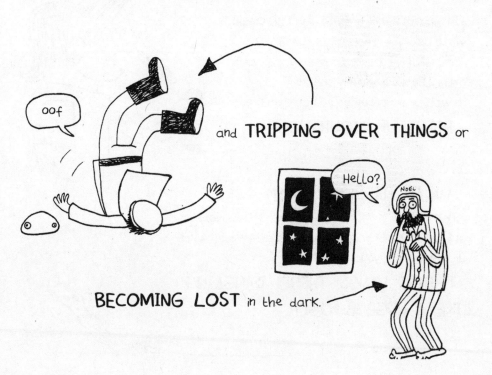

and **TRIPPING OVER THINGS** or

BECOMING LOST in the dark.

33

At the very top of the list of bathroom dangers is

THE TOOTHBRUSH SNAKE.

Belgium

This is an extremely rare and dangerous animal from Belgium. It looks like a toothbrush and is known to sneak into bathrooms and lie in wait by the sink.

If you are not paying full attention when you put toothpaste on it and start to lift it up toward your teeth, the toothbrush snake will leap from your hand and go

RIGHT UP YOUR NOSE.

WHAT HAPPENS THEN?

Then—and in many ways this is the worst part of a toothbrush-snake attack—it doesn't disappear up your nose,

IT JUST HANGS THERE, DANGLING LIKE A HUGE BOOGER.

HOW DO I GET RID OF THE
TOOTHBRUSH SNAKE?

Now this is tricky. You can't pull it out or try to get it down
with a vacuum cleaner because it really wedges itself up there.
It doesn't react to tickles and you can't blow it out, the way
you would with a booger.

No, the only way to get rid of a toothbrush snake is with **MUSIC.**
But music from the radio won't work. You have to play the music
yourself through a trumpet or one of the other instruments
you blow into.

DIAGRAM 1: The toothbrush
snake attacks.

DIAGRAM 2: Removing the
toothbrush snake.

BUT BEWARE!

Toothbrush snakes **REALLY HATE LOVE SONGS.**
It's best to play a national anthem or "Happy Birthday" or
something like that.

OK. How are you after that? Not **TOO FRIGHTENED** I hope, because let me tell you, this book is about to get a lot more terrifying **RIGHT NOW.**

DANGER PETS

Choosing the correct pet is a very important decision. Get it right and you have a new best friend.

Get it wrong and you have bought yourself a
**ONE-WAY TICKET TO CHOMPYTOWN,
IF YOU KNOW WHAT I MEAN**
(what I mean is that it could eat you).

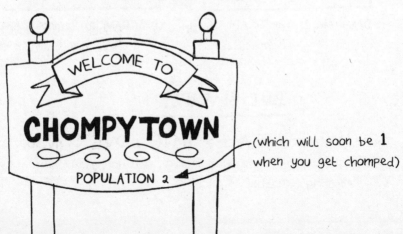

WELCOME TO

CHOMPYTOWN

POPULATION 2

(which will soon be **1** when you get chomped)

The most important question you need to ask yourself about any new pet is:

YES, IT LOOKS CUTE NOW, BUT WHAT WILL IT BE LIKE IN A YEAR?

With a new kitten, for example.

HOW CAN I BE SURE THIS CAT IS AN ORDINARY CAT AND NOT A BABY TIGER?

MEOW!

HOW TO CHECK IF YOUR CAT IS A TIGER

Ask yourself these three simple questions:

1. Is my cat much bigger than everyone else's cat?

2. Does it have very large teeth and sometimes try to eat the juiciest neighbors?

3. Instead of **MEOW**, does it go **ROAAARRRRRR** so loud that saucepans rattle and pictures on the walls go sideways? Except when there is a show about tigers on television, when it watches its friends silently, with tears in its eyes.

If you answered **YES** to any **TWO** of these questions, **THEN YOUR CAT IS DEFINITELY A BABY TIGER.** You should telephone your local zoo **IMMEDIATELY.** And, while you are waiting for them to arrive, **DANCE!**

(This Is A Tiger Alert! TIATA! TIATA!)

IS MY DOG A BABY WOLF?

Does it **HOOOOWWWWWLL** at
the moon? Does it really like chickens?
Are chickens going missing in your area?
Does your dog sometimes sneak out at
night and have lots of feathers stuck
to it in the morning and smell like chickens?

NEWSFLASH: THEN THAT IS NOT A DOG! TIAWA!

IS MY PET FISH A BABY GREAT WHITE SHARK?

Does it get really, really excited when
you eat a sandwich in front of it?
When it's hungry, does it swim along with
its top fin sticking out of the water?
Has it ever smashed out of its tank
and eaten a member of your family?

THEN YELL "TIASA!" AND HIRE AN OLD SEA CAPTAIN/SHARK FISHERMAN TO CATCH IT BEFORE IT CHOMPS ANYONE ELSE!

YARRR

39

IS MY HAMSTER A BABY HIPPOPOTAMUS?

Is it **MUCH** too big for its hamster wheel?

Is your hamster bigger than **YOU**?

Does it eat all of its dinner with one mighty chomp and then burp louder than a motorcycle?

not a hamster

a hamster

THEN I'M PRETTY SURE THAT IS NOT A HAMSTER. TIAHA!

Also **RAD!** Also **RUN AWAY NOW!**

Maybe you should consider getting a pet that poses

NO DANGER AT ALL—what, in DANGEROLOGY,

is known as an **ANDAAP** (Absolutely-Not-Dangerous-At-All Pet).

EXAMPLES OF SOME ANDAAPs

1. A HOUSE PLANT

It won't chew up your furniture or pee on your bed.
A house plant is like a dog that doesn't move around or
need dinner or do anything. Except grow, very slowly.

WARNING: A banana plant is a bad idea, though. **CHIMPS**
could hear about it **AND COME TO LIVE WITH YOU.**

WARNING 2: Avoid

HUMAN-EATING PLANTS
and be careful of

THE ARMCHAIR CACTUS,
which can also inflict great pain.

Time to relax

41

2. A CABBAGE

An excellent alternative to a pet. I love cabbages almost
as much as I love safety. The most delicious cabbages
I've ever tasted come from my next-door neighbor Gretel's shop,

GRETEL'S CABBAGE CABIN.

I go in there every day to get one for my lunch.
She is always so kind and friendly and always asks me
how I am. But I get shy and never end up saying anything.
I'm pretty sure I get nervous because of the risk of her
cabbage display falling down

AND US ALL GETTING
TRAPPED BENEATH A
CABBALANCHE

(a cabbage avalanche).

ADVICE: To stop your pet cabbage from getting smelly, keep it in
the fridge. Smelly cabbage is **NAAD**.

ADVICE 2: Don't eat your pet cabbage for lunch by mistake.
Even if it is **RED**.

3. A STONE

My pet of choice is a stone. It doesn't get hungry and you don't ever have to let it out to pee. Stones require very little looking after. Add some googly eyes and take it out for a walk whenever you want on a roller skate. This is my pet stone, Dennis.

I've had him for five years. He used to have a sister called Megan. But Megan got lost when I took them swimming at the beach. Dennis misses her very much. Look how sad he is, just thinking about her.

We hope to find her one day. She's somewhere out there.

Dennis

Dennis and Megan

She's still somewhere out there.

DANGER IN THE SKY

KITE FLYING

My nieces Katherine and Millicent love to come and stay with me.
Look at their happy faces!

I am trying to teach them about **DANGEROLOGY**,

but they don't seem to want to be **PODs**.
This is because they are too young to realize that

DANGER
IS
EVERYWHERE

For example, they love to fly their kites,

WHICH IS ONE OF THE MOST DANGEROUS THINGS YOU CAN DO.

I mean, what if:

1. The kite gets hit by lightning.

2. The kite gets picked up by an eagle.

3. The wind is too strong and lifts you up and drops you out at sea.

BUT a few BASIC SAFETY TIPS can make kite flying safe and fun.

1. NEVER FLY YOUR KITE WHEN IT IS WINDY.

Only when there is no wind at all. That way it won't be able to fly and

THERE IS NO DANGER.

2. Cut holes in your kite. This is another excellent way to

make sure it won't fly. **Or,** safer still, why not get rid of the kite, and tie the string on to a cabbage?

(PERHAPS A DELICIOUS CABBAGE FROM GRETEL'S CABBAGE CABIN.)

A Cabbage Kite

3. To make sure you are not blown away, MAKE YOURSELF AS HEAVY AS POSSIBLE. WEAR ALL OF YOUR CLOTHES.

Put your pet stone and any other heavy things you can find in your pockets. Eat a very large meal before you go out. You could even ask somebody to bury you in the ground up to your waist.

4. Better still, why not sit in the back seat of a car **WITH YOUR SEAT BELT ON** and fly the kite out the window or sunroof?

NOTE: BE CAREFUL, THOUGH. There is still a danger of **LOW-FLYING AIRCRAFT.**

What I recommend is that you **STAY AT HOME,** lie on your bed, and **PRETEND THAT YOU ARE FLYING A KITE.** You can even stick a piece of cardboard to the end of a broom. Look how much Katherine and Millicent are enjoying themselves!

THANKS, LADIES.

DANGER AT SCHOOL

IS MY TEACHER A VAMPIRE?

Vampires used to be easy to spot with their pointy capes/hair/teeth. But they realized this, and now dress much less vampirey, more like newscasters.

School is a perfect place for zombies and, in particular,

VAMPIRES to strike, so while you are there,

ALWAYS BE LOFDing.

A common vampire trick is to arrive at your school

POSING AS A NEW TEACHER.
"Oh, Mr/Ms. Your Normal Teacher can't come in today

(REAL REASON: BECAUSE I CHOMPED THEM),

so I will take over until they come back **(NEVER)."**

There are five ways of finding out if your new teacher is a vampire:

1. GARLIC

It is well known that vampires **HATE** garlic. So, why not give your new teacher **A GARLICKY WELCOME GIFT?**

Maybe garlic bread, or a chicken kiev, or a fruit basket where you have replaced all the fruit with bulbs of garlic.

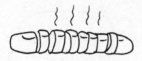 

If they are delighted and thank you for being so thoughtful, then you have welcomed your new teacher to the school with a nice welcome gift. If they run from the school screaming, then

CONGRATULATIONS!
YOU HAVE SAVED EVERYONE FROM A VAMPIRE.

2. PAPER EATING

Does your teacher eat paper? I don't mean chew on a little bit, I mean rip out pages and stuff them into his/her mouth.

Do books often go missing, and afterward does your teacher look full?

HAVE YOU EVER SEEN YOUR TEACHER FOLD UP PAGES AND PUT THEM INTO THEIR LUNCHTIME SOUP OR SANDWICH?

Well, then your teacher is definitely a vampire. Vampires love to eat paper.

It's why they are so pale.

3. SPARKLING WATER

Another less well-known fact about vampires is their reaction to sparkling/fizzy/bubbly water. It is not uncommon for sparkling water to make the drinker a bit burpy.

But if a vampire drinks sparkling water it makes them farty.

REALLY FARTY.

Not farty like the loudest fart you've ever had, though. Farty like the sound a ship makes when it is at sea and wants to say hello to another ship or a lighthouse.

Or when a huge truck wants to overtake another huge truck on the freeway.

Or when a vampire drinks sparkling water and farts.

4. A VERY EVIL LAUGH

A good way to spot a vampire is by their very evil laugh.

I, like most people, laugh like this: **Ha ha ha ha.**

Or sometimes like this: **Heh heh heh.**
I've heard Gretel laugh in the Cabbage Cabin, and she

laughs more like this: **Heeeeee heeeeee.**
What a nice laugh.
But vampires don't laugh like that. They laugh like this:

MWAHAHAHAHAHAHAHA.

And they really keep going with the **HAHAHAHAHA** part for ages.

MWAHAHAHAHAHAHAHAHAHAHAHAHAHAHAHAHAHAHAHAHAHAHAHA!
So try a joke out on your teacher and have a stopwatch ready.

You: Excuse me, Ms. Nightstalker?
Ms. Nightstalker: Yes, student.
You: Why did the soup have a black belt?
Ms. Nightstalker: Why, student?

You: Because it was a carroty **(SAY IT LIKE "KARATE")** soup.

Now start timing with the stopwatch.

MWAHAHAHAHAHAHAHAHAH . . .

If that laugh goes beyond ten seconds

THEN GET OUT OF THERE BECAUSE
MS. NIGHTSTALKER IS A VAMPIRE.

5. TURNING INTO A BAT

Finally, the best way you can tell if your teacher is a vampire is if they ever turn into a bat. Vampires can't drive and generally don't take the bus, so they either travel by turning into a bat **OR BY SEGWAY.**

ASK YOURSELF THE FOLLOWING QUESTIONS:

A. HAVE YOU EVER SEEN YOUR TEACHER TURN INTO A BAT AT THE END OF SCHOOL?

B. DID YOUR TEACHER EVER TURN UP LATE FOR SCHOOL AND WERE THEY A BAT?

C. DOES YOUR TEACHER COME TO SCHOOL ON A SEGWAY?

If you answered **YES** to any of these questions,

THEN YOUR TEACHER IS DEFINITELY A VAMPIRE.

Quick, go and tell your principal immediately!

No, wait. **FIRST MAKE SURE THAT YOUR PRINCIPAL ISN'T A VAMPIRE, TOO.**

WELL DONE!

You are extremely brave to have made it this far.
But I'm afraid if you think you are past the scary,
dangerous part **YOU COULD NOT BE MORE WRONG.**
We are only on page 53, and in this book,

just as **IN THE WORLD,**

DANGER ~ IS ~ EVERYWHERE

WE CONTINUE WITH OUR FIRST LIST OF

Top Ten Tips For Avoiding Danger In Everyday Situations

IN A VERY DANGEROUS PLACE.

TTTFADIES

AT THE SUPERMARKET

1. Plan your trip **CAREFULLY. Draw a DETAILED MAP** of the store with the sections you plan to visit and your estimated arrival time in each section.

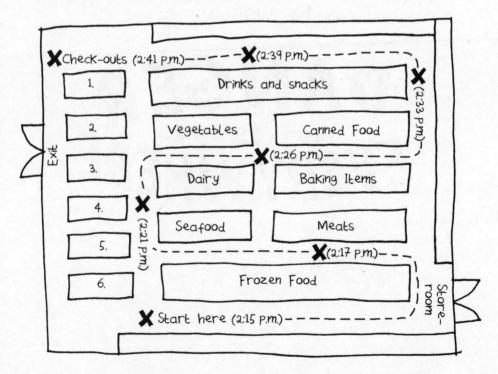

2. Carry out **A ROLL CALL** in each section to make sure all members of your shopping group have arrived

SAFELY AND ON TIME.

3. Avoid losing any members of your group by linking everyone with a long piece of rope. Make sure everyone has their name written on the back of their **T-COD**. This is in case you need to be addressed directly by an in-store announcement.

For example: "Could the man with **DOCTER NOEL ZONE** written on his hood, who has climbed on top of the pumpkins and is now scanning the shop with binoculars, please climb down?"

IT'S NOT A HOOD, IT'S A T-COD!

4. Select a cart with **FOUR WORKING WHEELS** and **NO WOBBLERS.** A wobbly wheel can affect steering and could cause **A MULTI-CART PILE-UP.** Add a pair of powerful bicycle lights to the front of the cart for **EXTRA VISIBILITY** and to find your way out of the shop in the event of a power outage. Push the cart with **GREAT CARE,** using hand signals and tooting your **DAD** when rounding corners.

Toot

5. BE CAREFUL around large product displays.

The slightest bump could topple it over and you could find yourself **TRAPPED UNDERNEATH** and have to **EAT YOUR WAY OUT.** This may be possible with a cabbalanche (which is a strange mixture of **TID** but also **RED**), but imagine eating your way out of a

MOUNTAIN OF LAUNDRY DETERGENT? (NAAD.)

— Toot

6. If you become unroped from the group and get lost in the supermarket,

DO NOT PANIC.

Simply follow the signs to the

HOUSEHOLD SECTION.

Then find the longest mop or broom and **PLACE YOUR T-COD ON THE END OF IT.**

Hoist the broom skywards, while sounding your **DAD.**

This should be easily spotted by the rest of your group.

Toot

7. In a very serious emergency, when
you have been lost for some time,
make your way to the

FIZZY DRINKS SECTION.

Find four of the

LARGEST BOTTLES OF
SPARKLING WATER,

shake them and place them directly
under your bottom.

Toot

When you open the lids,

YOU WILL
BE PROPELLED INTO
THE AIR ON A
FOUNTAIN OF FIZZ.

While you are up there, you
will be able to see where the
rest of your group is.

8. Avoid buying **VERY DANGEROUS THINGS,** such as really pointy turnips or lobsters that may still be alive.

Also beware of **SUPERMARKET LEOPARDS.** Their spotty, yellow fur means that they can easily hide underripe bananas.

BE READY WITH A DANCE (TIALA!).

9. The check-out area poses great danger, particularly for the shorter shopper. It is very easy to become mingled with the shopping and get packed up and sent home with other people.

IMAGINE IF THEY WEREN'T PAYING ATTENTION WHEN THEY GOT HOME AND PUT YOU STRAIGHT INTO A CASSEROLE!

EXCUSE ME!

To prevent this, keep repeating:

"I AM NOT A BAG OF CARROTS! I AM NOT A BAG OF CARROTS!"
and:

"I AM NOT A LEG OF LAMB! I AM NOT A LEG OF LAMB!"
when in the bagging area.

10. DO NOT OVERFILL YOUR BAGS.

Items could fall out, break open, and mix together, creating dangerous, new compounds. For example, eggs, dishwasher liquid, and cat food are all fine on their own, but put them together and they form a liquid that is so slippery

THE STORE WILL HAVE TO BE CLOSED

FOR A WEEK until it dries out.

If frosting, soda, and certain kinds of smelly cheese mix, they form a glue that is so strong **THAT IF YOU STAND IN IT YOU WILL HAVE TO ABANDON YOUR FOOTWEAR** and get **AIRLIFTED OUT** by **CRANE OR HELICOPTER.**

As a **DANGEROLOGIST**, I dedicate my life to **LOFDing**, **POWDMBing**, and **MSTDIDWEEIPSTIAing**. However, sometimes to get rid of danger, you have to put yourself in danger.

SOMETIMES THAT DANGER IS VERY GREAT.

For example,

BEE DANGER

People might say that the best thing to do with a bee in your home is to ignore it. Just open the window and it will find its own way out. To these people I say:

ARE YOU NUTS?
THINK OF ALL THE PANIC AND MAYHEM
A BEE CAN CAUSE WHEN IT'S FLYING
AROUND YOUR HOME!

Examples of panic and mayhem a bee can cause when it's flying around your home:

1. Distracting you and causing accidents.

2. STING! STING! STING!

3. Flying into your ear and getting stuck inside your brain.

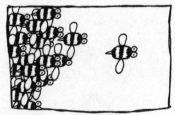

4. Signaling to millions of its friends to come in.

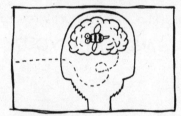

5. WHAT IF IT'S NOT A BEE BUT A WASP IN A BEE DISGUISE?

HOW TO REMOVE A BEE FROM YOUR HOME

There are many ways to get rid of a bee, but they are all

VERY DANGEROUS.

You can put on your suit of armor and try to hit it with a
swatter or spray it with a spray.

But you could easily have an **ACCIDENT WHILE YOU
ARE RUNNING** around after it.

YOU COULD GET A BEE-EATING LIZARD.

But what if that turns out to be a **BABY DINOSAUR
AND EATS YOU?**

No, there is only one safe way to get rid of a bee.

You have to **PRETEND TO BE A BEE, TOO**. But not an
ordinary bee. Bees don't listen to other ordinary bees.

Bees only listen to **THE QUEEN BEE.**

QUEEN-BEE DISGUISE

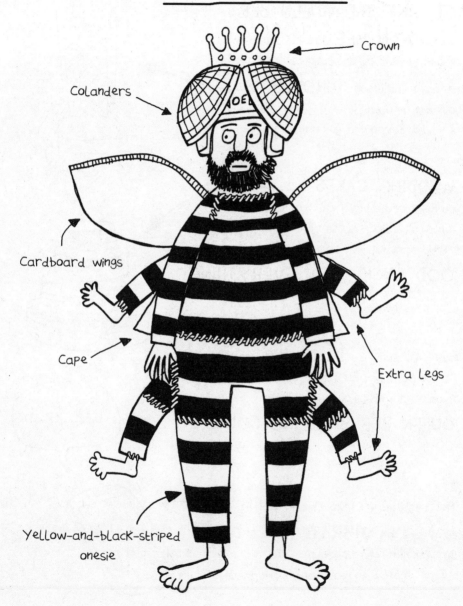

Crown

Colanders

Cardboard wings

Cape

Extra Legs

Yellow-and-black-striped onesie

With the correct outfit, now you have to

ACT LIKE THE QUEEN BEE.

The **QUEEN BEE** doesn't land on ordinary tables or fridges.

She only lands on **THRONES** _____ (you will probably need to borrow a throne)

and

WEDDING CAKES _____

(you will probably need to borrow a wedding cake unless you are getting married—if so,

GOOD LUCK WITH EVERYTHING).

Finally to convince the bee that you are an actual queen bee, you need to make a very loud

QUEEN-BEE BUZZING SOUND.

BZZZZZZ!

The best way to do this is with a cell phone on **VIBRATE**.

So you need to organize lots of people to call and text you.

After an hour of moving between the wedding cake and the throne, simply say **"LET'S GO!"** and walk out the front door of your house. If the bee doesn't follow you **THEN IT IS A WASP IN DISGUISE AND YOU WILL HAVE TO MOVE OUT OF YOUR HOUSE UNTIL IT IS GONE.**

NOTE: Don't spend too long standing outside in your queen-bee costume. A neighbor might think you are a **HUGE BEE** and try to spray you or hit you with a very large swatter.

This would be **REALLY EMBARRASSING IF THAT NEIGHBOR WAS GRETEL.**

Welcome

TO THE

DANGERZONE

(PART 1)

Now that we are getting to know each other,
it's time Dennis and I showed you around our home,
which we call **THE DANGERZONE**.

We will begin outside with:

THE DANGERYARD.

Here is Dennis showing you the front:

Here is Dennis showing you the back:

That's right. There is nothing in our yard. I have covered
it all with cement. This means:
- There is nowhere for danger to lurk.
- It's impossible for dangerous animals to tunnel underneath
  and surprise us.
  - There are **NO RAPID-GROWING TREES OR PLANTS**
    that could suddenly fill the yard and trap us in our house.

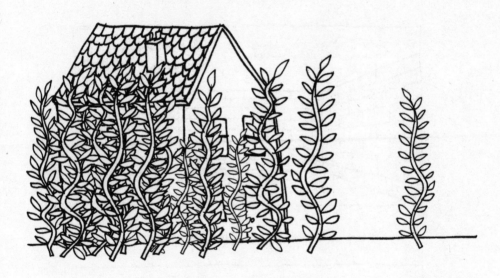

BUT WHY ARE THERE SO MANY LEAVES IN MY YARD?

An excellent question. **GOOD QUESTIONING.**

This is because I have

THE WORST NEIGHBORS IN THE
HISTORY OF NEIGHBORS.

(I am certainly **NOT** talking about Gretel here.)
At the back of my yard is the giraffe enclosure at the zoo.
They stare, they litter, they make strange giraffe-chewing
sounds while staring and littering. I have written to the
zoo thirty-one times to complain about their behavior, but

DO THEY MOVE THE GIRAFFES TO ANOTHER
PART OF THE ZOO?

 # NO!

They leave them where they are and feed them my
complaint letters. I know this because sometimes the
giraffes drop my half-eaten complaint letters back into

THE DANGERYARD.

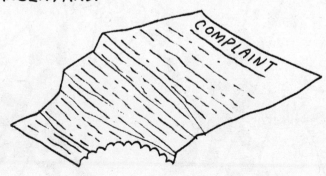

STOP STARING AT ME, GIRAFFES.

YOU WEIRD STRETCHY HORSES.

My neighbors on one side are David and Chris.
I'm not sure what they do, because they are always
around. So probably something to do with computers.

Chris ——————▶   ◀—————— David

They used to have a pond in their backyard until it got
filled in, which is lucky because

A CROCODILE COULD HAVE COME TO LIVE IN IT.

And it would have chomped David and Chris. And then me.

AND THEN GRETEL. SO IT IS VERY GOOD THAT IT
GOT FILLED IN. REALLY, REALLY GOOD.

OK, OK.
 I admit it.

  I filled it in. ——————▶

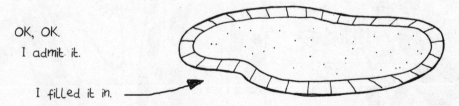

That is actually how we met. It was very late, and they
heard an unusual sound coming from their yard
(me, filling in their pond) and called the police.
Although David and Chris were very understanding when
I explained about the crocodile, the policewoman was
not, and she told me that I'll be in big trouble if I'm
caught in a neighbor's yard without their permission again.

On the other side of my house lives the very beautiful
and wonderful **GRETEL**.

She is much
prettier than
this.

She grows cabbages in her garden.

Whenever she sees me on the road, she always
says hello. But I'm never sure what to say, so I hide.
Which is a difficult thing to do when I am in my yard.

I wish I didn't panic and just said hello back.
I would tell her that, in addition to burrowing animals
and fast-growing mutant cabbages that could trap her in
her house, there are other

AWFUL DANGERS IN HER YARD

I would talk to her about:

1. How dangerous bicycles are.
2. How she could become trapped in her hammock.
3. How her barbecue is too close to her house and could set everything on fire.
4. How her birdfeeder could **ATTRACT VULTURES.**
5. The danger of leaving things outside when there could be snow. They might get covered and

GRETEL COULD EASILY TRIP OVER SOMETHING.

GRETEL'S YARD

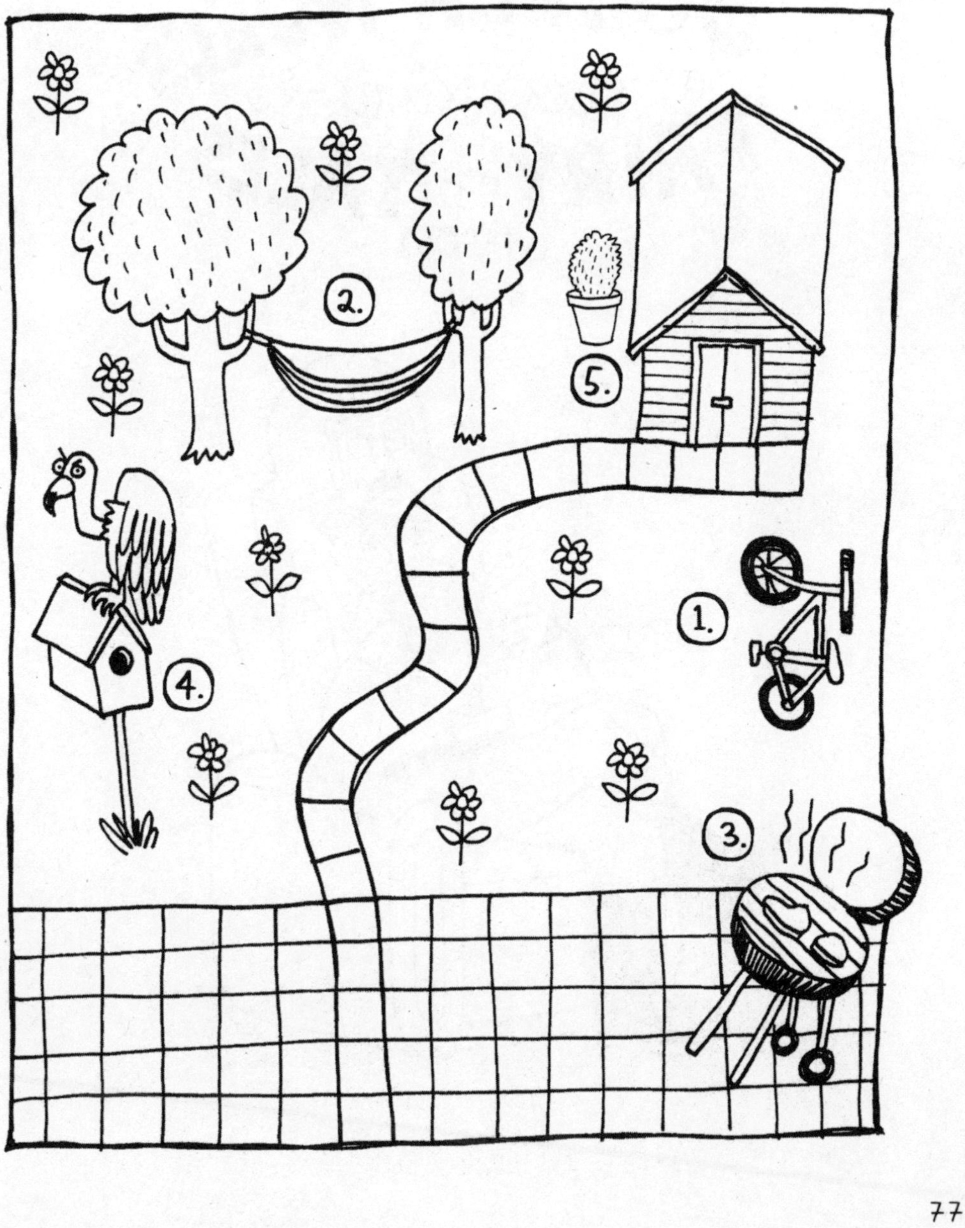

1.
2.
3.
4.
5.

DOCTER NOEL'S

Relaxing

FAIRY TALES

(WAFOS)

WELL DONE FOR READING THE BOOK THIS FAR.

I hope you are remembering everything for the **DETBAFOD.**

You deserve a break, so I have rewritten a classic fairy tale for you to enjoy **WITH A FOCUS ON SAFETY.**

PLEASE ENJOY IT.

Little Red Riding Hood →

Once upon a time, Little Red Riding Hood decided that she would visit her grandmother who lived in a cottage across the forest. She thought about how she might get there. She could walk through the forest. But then she realized

THAT THIS WAS A TERRIBLE IDEA because forests are full of angry squirrels and hairy spiders. And, even if she didn't meet any of them, she could **WALK INTO A TREE.**

She thought about riding her bike on the well-lit bike path through the middle of the forest,

BUT THEN REMEMBERED HOW DANGEROUS BICYCLES ARE. And how **AWFUL IT WOULD BE** if the chain fell off or she scraped her knee **AND A PANTHER/WOLF/HIPPO HAD ESCAPED FROM THE ZOO AND WAS ON THE LOOSE IN THE FOREST (TIAPA/TIAWA/TIAHA!).**

She could ask her father to drive her on the road that went around the forest,

BUT WHAT IF THERE WAS A POLICE CHASE WITH PEOPLE SHOOTING GUNS FROM CARS?

So, in the end, Little Red Riding Hood decided to call Grandma and tell her that she wasn't going to make it today, because everything was too dangerous.

"Oh, well," said her grandmother.
"It would have been very nice to see you."
And as Little Red Riding Hood went to put the phone down,
it fell on her foot and gave her a bruise because
she was just wearing socks.

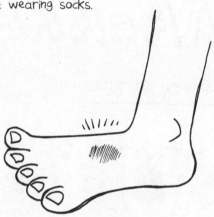

MORAL: NEVER GO AROUND IN JUST YOUR SOCKS

because

DANGE
IS
EVERYV

Th

Now get ready to toot your **DAD** for our first
Advice About Avoiding Angry and Aggressive Animal Attacks.

AAAAaAAA

THE POLAR BEAR

or work or to buy a cabbage—
but in front of you.

O?

Because polar bears can run and swim faster than you, are better at climbing trees, and have an excellent sense of smell, you might think that you have no chance of escaping from one.

And you are right. But what you can do is **AMAZE THEM**. And, while they are still amazed, sneak away.

HOW DO I AMAZE A POLAR BEAR?

Two words: **CARD TRICKS.**

Polar bears love card tricks. And they are so bamboozled by even the most basic one they will sit there, for up to an hour, trying to work out how it was done.

1. You meet a polar bear.

2. Quickly remove a pack of cards from your PEBB.

3. Do a card trick.

4. Polar bear is amazed.

5. THIS IS YOUR OPPORTUNITY TO RUN AWAY! QUICKLY. RUN!

I am warning you now, even by experienced

FOD standards, this next one is really frightening.

GRANNY, DANGER

Most people would put Granny at the bottom of the list of family members who might cause danger.

LIST OF FAMILY MEMBERS WHO MIGHT CAUSE DANGER

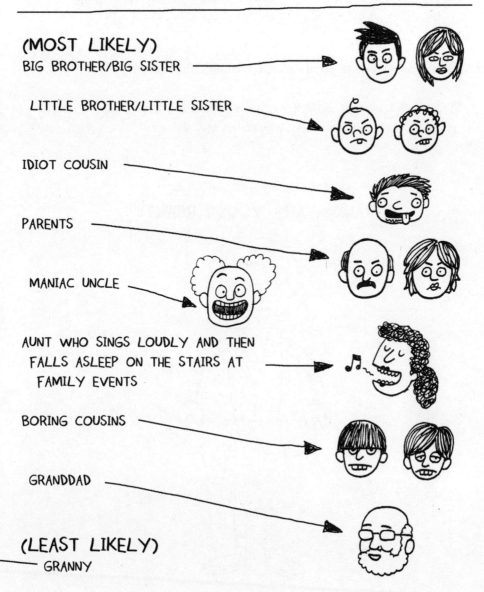

(MOST LIKELY)
BIG BROTHER/BIG SISTER

LITTLE BROTHER/LITTLE SISTER

IDIOT COUSIN

PARENTS

MANIAC UNCLE

AUNT WHO SINGS LOUDLY AND THEN
FALLS ASLEEP ON THE STAIRS AT
FAMILY EVENTS

BORING COUSINS

GRANDDAD

(LEAST LIKELY)
GRANNY

There are many questions we love to ask our grandparents:

"Did you ever go to school on a horse?"

"Why didn't you go to the moon with Neil Armstrong?"

"Before the remote control was invented, did you sit on the couch and poke the buttons on the TV with a long stick?"

But one we fail to ask very often is:

"GRANNY, ARE YOU A ROBOT?"

WHAT IS A ROBOT GRANNY?

A robot granny is a robot that has been built by other robots to look like your real granny.

HOW DOES THIS HAPPEN?

The usual trick of the robots is to distract your real granny by

HAVING A FREE TASTING OF FOOD AT THE SUPERMARKET.

Robots (disguised as humans) will offer food samples that grannies enjoy, such as:
fruitcake,
weird soup,
and fresh prunes/prune juice/
  bars with prunes in them.

Tasting stands at the supermarket delay the average granny for thirty minutes. This is all the time that the robots need to

BUILD A ROBOT COPY OF YOUR GRANNY.

This robot granny then comes over to your home and
suggests that you go to the park or the beach,
SOMEWHERE WITH LARGE OPEN SPACES to play with a
dog she is watching.

(NOTE: DOG IS ALSO A ROBOT.)

But, when you get there and go to throw the stick
for the dog, suddenly...

WHOOSH,

a robot spaceship swoops down
and grabs you with a grabbing claw.
Like one of those machines where you
never win anything. Next they pull
you up into their spaceship and take
you back to their robot planet.

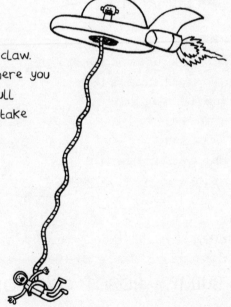

WHAT HAPPENS THERE?

They make you live in a **HUMAN ZOO**, which is exactly like one of our zoos **BUT WITH HUMANS INSTEAD OF ANIMALS.** Robots come with their families and watch you do boring human stuff like **EAT, SLEEP, AND PLAY WITH A TIRE HANGING FROM A TREE.** Which is fun for a while, but gets really boring. Also the only food they think we like is carrots, which, again, is fine for a while, but you get so sick of them.

HOW CAN I PREVENT THIS FROM HAPPENING?

You need to make sure that your granny is your actual granny and not a robot. One way is to ask her to do something that only your real granny could do:

"Hey, Granny, teach me your favorite kind of dancing, please." ⟶

Or

"Granny, what is that cake you make that I really like? And please show me how to make it."

If she can't do the dance, or if she tries to make the cake but it doesn't taste right, **SHE MAY BE A ROBOT.** Ask to see her watch. All robots have an on/off button located **UNDERNEATH THEIR WATCH.** So if there's a button under there, hold it down for three seconds and your robot granny will power off. Then wait for your real granny to come back from the supermarket.

That robot will be in **HUGE** trouble.

Thank you.

To those brave readers who are still reading, if you can stay all the way to the end,

YOU WILL MAKE TRULY EXCELLENT FODs.

To those less brave readers who have been scared away already, I say . . . well, I don't say anything because they aren't reading anymore. But I would say:

SCHOOL TRIP DANGER

Let me set the scene. You've been on a bus all day
with your classmates. Somebody has eaten too much
chocolate and been sick, somebody else has gotten lost,
and you've driven for ages to spend an hour listening
to a very old lady talk very quietly about a castle

THAT COULD COLLAPSE AT ANY MINUTE.

Then on the way back to the school, just when you

think it couldn't get any worse, it gets **MUCH** worse.

THE BUS IS AMBUSHED BY PIRATES.

The usual pirate trick is to pretend they are working on the road. Yellow hard hats and bright orange coats conceal their piratey outfits.

One of them holds out a **STOP** sign and when the driver opens the door to speak to them ten more pirates rush onboard.

WHAT TO DO IF PIRATES TAKE OVER YOUR SCHOOL BUS

1. NOBODY MENTION GOLD or TREASURE. That is what they are looking for. Don't even mention it in passing. Don't even say "My favorite bird is a goldfinch," or "My cousin is called Marigold."

2. SAY PIRATEY THINGS. If you try to sound like a pirate, they will be friendlier to you, like if you try to speak French when you're on vacation in France.

Walk the Plank!

Ahoy, me Hearties!

Bonjour!

HOW TO SOUND LIKE A PIRATE

Instead of **"hello,"** say **"yarrrr,"** and instead of all other words say **"arrr."**

So, **"Hello! I hope you are having a nice day,"** becomes **"Yarrrr! Arrr arrr arrr arrr arrr arrr arrr arrr."**

3. The way to get rid of pirates is very simple. You just need to give them a map. Tell them you found it hidden in an old book. Don't worry if you don't have a real one—you can draw one. Add in stuff that pirates will recognize, like a forest, a bandana shop, and a sushi restaurant (Pirates **LOVE** sushi).

Then, **AND THIS IS THE KEY,** put a large **X** somewhere on the map. As soon as the pirates see that, they will abandon your bus to go off to find this buried treasure.

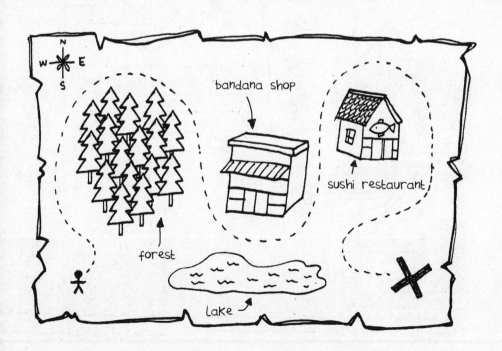

bandana shop

sushi restaurant

forest

lake

I think this next section could be why Mr. Donohoe has barred me from his bike shop.

DANGER ON WHEELS

Take a look at my list of the most dangerous ways to travel.

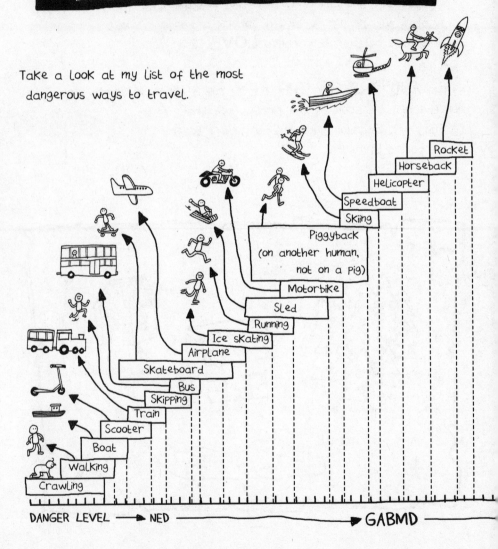

DANGER LEVEL → NED ————————→ GABMD

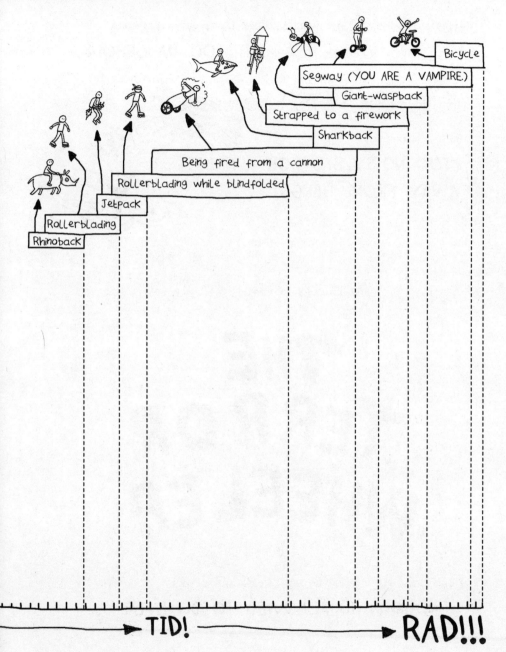

Bicycle

Segway (YOU ARE A VAMPIRE.)

Giant-waspback

Strapped to a firework

Sharkback

Being fired from a cannon

Rollerblading while blindfolded

Jetpack

Rollerblading

Rhinoback

TID! ➔ RAD!!!

If I was in charge, the world would be a very different place. There would be no weekends (**TOO DANGEROUS**),

no toffee **(TOO CHEWY)**,

no flip-flops
(TOO NOISY/BAD FOR RUNNING AWAY FROM THINGS).

And I would rename the bicycle to

THE TERROR WHEELER

and put cycling on my list of things that
NOBODY IS ALLOWED TO DO EVER.

WHY ARE BICYCLES SO DANGEROUS?

Well, if you hadn't noticed already,

BICYCLES DON'T MAKE ANY SENSE.

You stand it up on its own, and it just falls over.
But you sit on it and turn the pedals and expect
it to hold you up?

I DON'T TRUST THEM AND YOU SHOULDN'T, EITHER.

Gretel has a bicycle with a big basket that she uses to
get the cabbages to the Cabbage Cabin every morning.

WHY, GRETEL?

WHY DO YOU RISK IT?

SOMETHING AWFUL COULD HAPPEN.

Gretel is even
prettier than this.

EXAMPLES OF AWFUL THINGS
THAT COULD HAPPEN TO GRETEL

1. She could fall off.

2. A wasp could fly down the front of her coat.

(GRETEL HAS SOME EXCELLENT COATS.)

3. A bee could fly into her mouth, and so every time she blows her nose honey comes out.

4. Her brakes could stop working and she could cycle into the **POISONOUS INSECTS SECTION OF THE ZOO.**

INSECTS

NOOOOOOO

5. Her brakes could stop working and she could cycle into the shop that sells plates and glasses and other small, expensive things that can easily break.

6. Her brakes could squeak and all the cats in the area (including tigers, panthers, leopards, etc.) would think she is a huge mouse and come to eat her.

7. A boxer could hear her bell and think it is the start of a boxing match.

8. She could cycle through somebody's washing line and end up with a sheet over her and people would think she was a ghost.

PLEASE BE CAREFUL, GRETEL.

DOCTER NOEL ZONE'S TIPS FOR BICYCLE SAFETY FOR GRETEL AND EVERYBODY ELSE

1.

Place your bicycle in a large box.

2.

Take the box to a very high sea cliff.

3.

Check that there is nobody standing at
the bottom of the cliff.

4.

5.

Throw the box off the cliff.

6.

Go home and **DON'T EVER THINK ABOUT GOING NEAR ANOTHER BICYCLE EVER AGAIN.**

Thank you.

HOMEWORK DANGER

We all know about **THE PAGE 9 SCORPION** (see page 9), but there are many other dreadful dangers to be aware of while doing your homework. Here are the awful top four:

1. SCHOOLBAG HEAD

It happens to hundreds of students every year. You get home and are really looking forward to tackling your homework. But, in your eagerness to find the right book, you shove your head too far into your schoolbag and it gets wedged in. Suddenly you can't see anything and nobody can hear your cries of distress.

The only cure for schoolbag head is to go to the hospital, where they can get it off with a special bicycle pump.

2. PENCIL-CASE INJURIES

Putting your hand into a pencil case is more dangerous than

PUTTING YOUR HAND INTO A SOCKFUL OF FURIOUS CRABS.

Pencil cases are filled with sharp things, which can easily poke you while you are rummaging. This is why I use a

STATIONERY SOMBRERO.

A large hat with everything I could possibly need hanging from it on strings. I simply turn the hat around to whatever item I require. It's useful, it's stylish—wear your stationery sombrero out and everybody will be staring at you jealously.

WARNING: NEVER RIDE A BIKE WHILE WEARING YOUR STATIONERY SOMBRERO!

Items could become detached and cause grave danger to passersby (unless passersby are zombies/werewolves).

Also, **NEVER RIDE A BIKE. TID/RAD!**

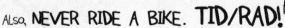

3. POINTY PENS AND PENCILS

Some people say that the pen is mightier than the sword.
All I know is that a sharp pencil is

JUST AS DANGEROUS AS A SWORD.

Remember to cover all pens and pencils with a **SAFETY SPROUT**

and a **PROTECTOR POTATO**. Especially those

ones hanging from your **STATIONERY SOMBRERO**.

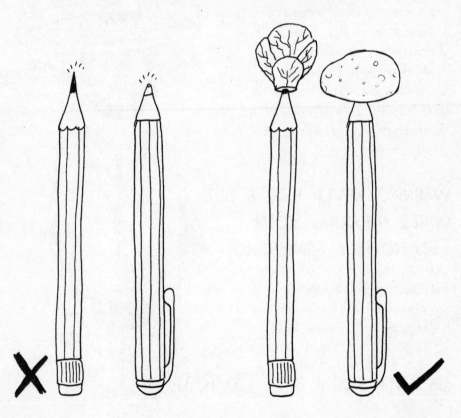

4. HAUNTED BOOKS

When working with old books you've borrowed from the library,

MAKE SURE THEY'RE NOT HAUNTED.

Haunted books are easy to spot because they are large, dusty, and make a loud creeeeeaaak sound when you open them. Reading aloud from a haunted book could **CAST A SPELL** and turn your dog into A **FRUIT/VEGETABLE.**

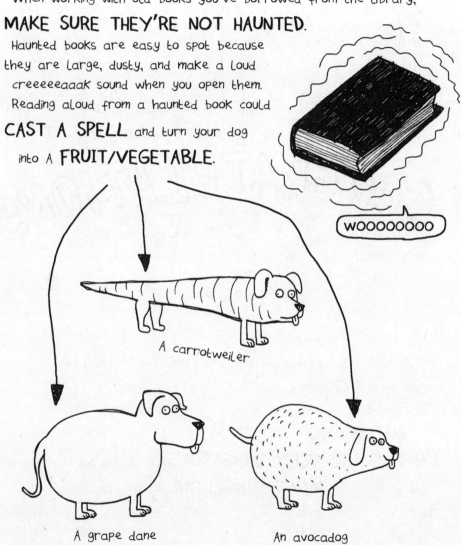

WOOOOOOOO

A carrotweiler

A grape dane

An avocadog

You are nearly halfway through this book, and halfway to

becoming a **FOD!**

This would be a good time to have a party to celebrate,

BUT DO NOT DO THIS!

PARTIES ARE VERY DANGEROUS. So dangerous that we will

now look at the **MOST DANGEROUS** variety of party.

TTTFADIES

BIRTHDAY PARTIES

It's hard to think of anything as dangerous as a birthday party. Maybe a version of *Romeo and Juliet*

WHERE JULIET IS PLAYED BY AN ANGRY SILVERBACK GORILLA.

(Not happy)

What starts off as a happy celebration so often ends
with somebody needing a bandage and somebody else
crying in a party hat.

Here are some essential party tips **(WAFOS):**

1. INVITATIONS

Invite as few people as possible. I would aim for none,
but one or two is acceptable. Remember the golden rule
for birthday-party guests:

"The more people you allow,
the more people will go owww."

NOEL

2. TIMING

Birthday parties always go on too long. Instead of 3:00 p.m. to 6:00 p.m., why not start it at 3:00 p.m. but end it at 3:30 p.m.?

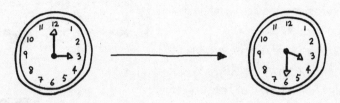

Or even better, 7:00 a.m to 7:05 a.m.

At that time nobody is awake enough to do anything dangerous.

Remember the golden rule for birthday-party length:

"The longer it goes on, the more things that can go wrong."

NOEL

113

3. PARTY ACTIVITIES

AVOID THE NORMAL PARTY ACTIVITIES.

Bowling, swimming, movies, and painting
are very dangerous.

Why not try a new and exciting
idea like sitting down beside a
nice hedge, or visiting a printer-ink
cartridge shop?

4. PRESENTS

Everybody loves a helmet. If the person
has a helmet already, why not get them
a new one. Maybe one that is big enough
to go on top of their old helmet.

(A double helmet.) ⟶

5. CAKE

Baking a cake could set your house on fire, so instead
of a cake use a cabbage, cut in half.
(Maybe a delicious one from

GRETEL'S CABBAGE CABIN.)

You can wear the other half
as a **COOL BIRTHDAY CROWN.**

6. CANDLES

Candles? HAS YOUR BRAIN FALLEN OUT AND BEEN REPLACED WITH A SWIMMING CAP FULL OF SAUSAGES?

Candles mean **FIRE**.

DO YOU WANT TO INVITE FIRE TO YOUR PARTY?

No, candles are much, much too dangerous. That's why I use carrots.

Carrots (pointy end up) look quite like candles, and they take forever to blow out. Also you can eat them when you're finished. So shove some carrots into your birthday cabbage, take it along to the hedge or printer-ink

cartridge shop, and **LET THE PARTY BEGIN!**

7. GAMES

Pin the Tail on the Donkey, with its combination of a sharp thing, a blindfold, and a picture of a lethal animal, is much too dangerous. Instead, why not play

PUT THE CABBAGE ON THE TABLE

8. MUSICAL CHAIRS

This should be called Musical Tears because of the number of things that can go wrong. So I propose some new rules to make it safer, but still a lot of fun.

RULE 1: Everyone needs to be wearing chair-pants.

WHAT ARE CHAIR-PANTS?

Chair-pants are the best sort of pants to wear for musical chairs. If you don't already own a pair, you can make some.

HOW DO I MAKE CHAIR-PANTS?

You will need:
- 1 chair
- 1 pair of pants
- 1 large bottle of glue

Directions:

STEP ONE: Glue the chair to the seat of your pants.

STEP TWO: That's it.

RULE 2: When the music starts, everyone slowly walks around in their chair-pants. **NOTE:** Choose a slow, sad song such as "Silent Night" or "Somewhere Over the Rainbow."

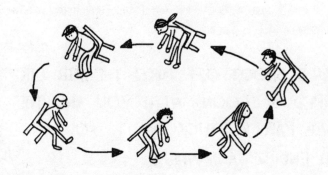

RULE 3: When the music stops, everyone sits down on their chair-pants.

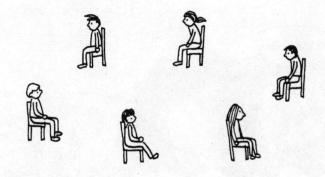

RULE 4: When the music starts, everyone walks slowly around again.

RULE 5: Continue this until going-home time.

9. NO BOUNCY CASTLES

Yes, falling over in a bouncy castle is less painful than falling over in a real castle. But think what would happen if the bouncy castle got a hole.

IT WOULD SHOOT OFF INTO THE AIR LIKE A POPPED BALLOON, WITH YOU AND THE WHOLE PARTY STUCK ON IT. YOU COULD END UP ANYWHERE. . . .

on a desert island

on top of a real castle

10. SURPRISE PARTIES

I don't like surprise parties because what if the person is **TOO SURPRISED** and faints with shock and bangs their head?

However, it is fun to organize some **NED** surprises as part of the party. For example:

SURPRISE!

I've poured all of the unhealthy fizzy drinks down the sink and now all we have to drink is cabbage juice!

SURPRISE!

You thought we were going to have a magician, but instead everyone has to lie down on the floor and take a nap!

SURPRISE!

This party is cancelled because parties are too dangerous. Everybody go home.

DRESSING FOR DANGER

So far in this book I am sure you have learned a huge
amount, but I'm sure you have also been impressed
by my unique style and fashion sense. I'm sure you
have said to yourself:

"THERE IS A MAN WHO LIKES TO BE SAFE, WHILE REMAINING 100% SNAZZY."

Very often when I get my
cabbage, Gretel remarks
on how shiny my helmet is
and how well I'm looking.
Although I never say anything
at the time, now I say:

"THANK YOU, GRETEL."

Many readers will probably want to start dressing like me,
so let me take you through

MY TOP FASHION DOS AND DON'TS.

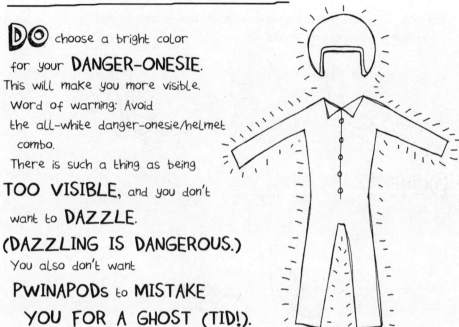

DO choose a bright color

for your **DANGER-ONESIE.**
This will make you more visible.
Word of warning: Avoid
the all-white danger-onesie/helmet
combo.
There is such a thing as being

TOO VISIBLE, and you don't

want to **DAZZLE.**

(DAZZLING IS DANGEROUS.)
You also don't want

PWINAPODs to **MISTAKE**

YOU FOR A GHOST (TID!).

DON'T combine a **BROWN ONESIE** with a

GREEN HELMET. To short-sighted animals, you will now
resemble a tree. Squirrels and birds may try to nest in you.

DON'T wear slip-on shoes. Or slippers. Or flippers.
Don't wear any shoes with the word "slip" or "flip" in their name.

Flipping, flopping, flippering, and slipping are exactly what
you don't want shoes to do.

DON'T wear any shoes with heels. Don't wear sandals.

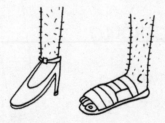

DON'T WEAR ANY SHOES WITH LACES.

An open lace TURNS A SHOE INTO A BANANA PEEL.

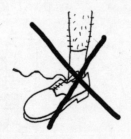

DO wear a good pair of waterproof rubber boots. And for special occasions wear slightly shinier rubber boots.

DON'T EVER WEAR A TIE.

It can dangle down and get stuck in things, dragging you into photocopiers/vacuum cleaners/lions **(TIALA!).**

DO maintain the smart appearance of a tie by wearing a T-shirt with a picture of a tie on it.

DON'T wear a full-length cape. That would be dangerous and ridiculous. However a **T-COD** alerts other dangerologists that you are one of them. I made mine out of a dish towel.

DO always carry your **PEBB**, containing essential **ADEGS** such as:

1. your **DAD** – to signal for attention

2. a spare **DAD** – in case your first **DAD** doesn't work

3. a cookie – to distract dangerous animals

4. a pack of cards – for polar bears

5. a bottle of bubble mixture **(WE WILL GET TO THIS LATER)**

6. a map – in case you get lost

7. an atlas – in case you get very lost

8. a globe – in case you get very, very lost

DO think about what dangers you may encounter that day when getting dressed in the morning. For example, if you will be in a high place (upstairs in a tall building or on a bus) you should wear a parachute. If you will be near a nippy dog, you should wear a suit of armor.

VIKING DANGER

If this book had been written one thousand years ago, it would have been one page long, and that page would have just said:

AAAAAGH, VIKINGS!

Vikings used to ruin **EVERYTHING**. You'd be finishing up building your house, putting in the very last pane of glass, when suddenly coming over the hill you'd see their pointy axes and helmets with the hair sticking out underneath.

Then you'd hear them roar:

SMA-SHE-ROO-NEE

And five minutes of **SMASH SMASH SMASH** later, your nice new house would be a mound of bricks and slate and broken glass.

One thousand years ago, you'd be on a camping trip, and you'd have just put the last bit of a really hard 800-piece jigsaw in, when suddenly you'd hear it:

SMA-SHE-ROO-NEE

And soon your tent would be as flat as a rug, and your jigsaw, and the folding camping table you were doing it on, would be a pile of broken folding camping table and jigsaw bits.

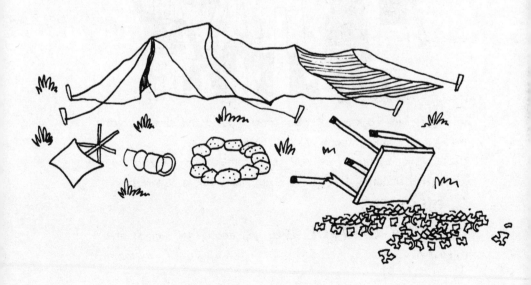

But that was one thousand years ago. Over time everyone heard about how much Vikings liked to smash things up.

Once you've heard about them, they're pretty easy to spot.

And soon everyone got to know their roar.

SMA-SHE-ROO-NEE

So people got locks for their front doors and stopped going camping when there were Vikings in the area.

These days, Vikings have had to become much sneakier to get to do the smashing they love. They now use a variety

of **DISGUISES**.

So be **VERY CAREFUL** when you encounter any of the following groups:

1. BANDS

Vikings tried posing as many different musical groups,
but it wasn't very convincing:

As boybands and girlbands—they
never quite got the look right.

As opera singers—they are
awful at singing.

As orchestras—they
kept smashing up their
little instruments.

As heavy metal bands—the
music was too loud,
even for them.

But then they found **FOLK MUSIC**.

Vikings look a bit like folk musicians anyway and can
strum and hit instruments just like folk musicians do.

So **BEWARE** if you see a folk band in concert or just performing at the side of the street.

THEY COULD BE HIDING
AXES AND HAMMERS BEHIND
THEIR BANJOS AND GUITARS.

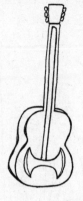
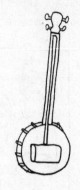

Listen very carefully in case their song suddenly goes:

SMA-SHE-ROO-NEE

and be ready to get out of there very quickly.

2. SCOUTS

Sometimes to get closer to the things they love to smash, Vikings will dress as the last people you'd expect to do any smashing. Take a close look at any Boy or Girl Scouts who come to your house to ask if you have any odd jobs they can help you with.

How does that Scout have a beard?

And isn't he a bit old to be doing this?

3. SANTAS

A common trick the Vikings try every Christmas Eve is to come to homes dressed as a group of Santas.

DO NOT, UNDER ANY CIRCUMSTANCES, EVER LET THEM IN!

Santa is supposed to work alone and come down the chimney,

NOT THROUGH THE FRONT DOOR WITH FOUR OF HIS TWIN BROTHERS/SISTERS.

And he is supposed to say

"HO HO HO!" not "SMA-SHE-ROO-NEE!"

4.

BIKING OR HIKING VIKINGS

There's a bunch of people
on bikes, or maybe all in their
hiking boots. Not an unusual
sight, you think to yourself. Maybe they
are all from the same club or team. But wait.
They don't look very fit.

AND WHY ARE THEY CARRYING AXES AND HAMMERS?

AAAAAGH.

THEY ARE BIKING OR HIKING VIKINGS, AND THEY ARE ABOUT TO START STRIKING!

NOTE: JUST BECAUSE I HAVE A BEARD DOES NOT MEAN THAT I AM A VIKING.

NOTE 2: IT ALSO DOES NOT MEAN THAT I AM A WEREWOLF.

The children from the school at the end of the road have a variety of names they call me as I walk past their yard with my cabbage every lunchtime.

It is the last one of these that bothers me most.
I, like many men, choose to have a beard because:

1. Shaving and razors = **RAD**

2. A beard is a **NATURAL FACE CUSHION** if I slip.

3. It makes me look quite handsome. (Gretel once told me that I have "a lovely beard.")

Thank you.

But it does **NOT** make me a werewolf.

5 REASONS WHY I AM DEFINITELY NOT A WEREWOLF

1. A werewolf is a **MYTHICAL BEAST** that is half man, half wolf. They go outside and **BECOME WOLFY** when there is a full moon. Whereas I stay **INSIDE** when there is any sort of moon **BECAUSE IT IS THE NIGHT AND THE NIGHT IS DARK AND DANGEROUS.**

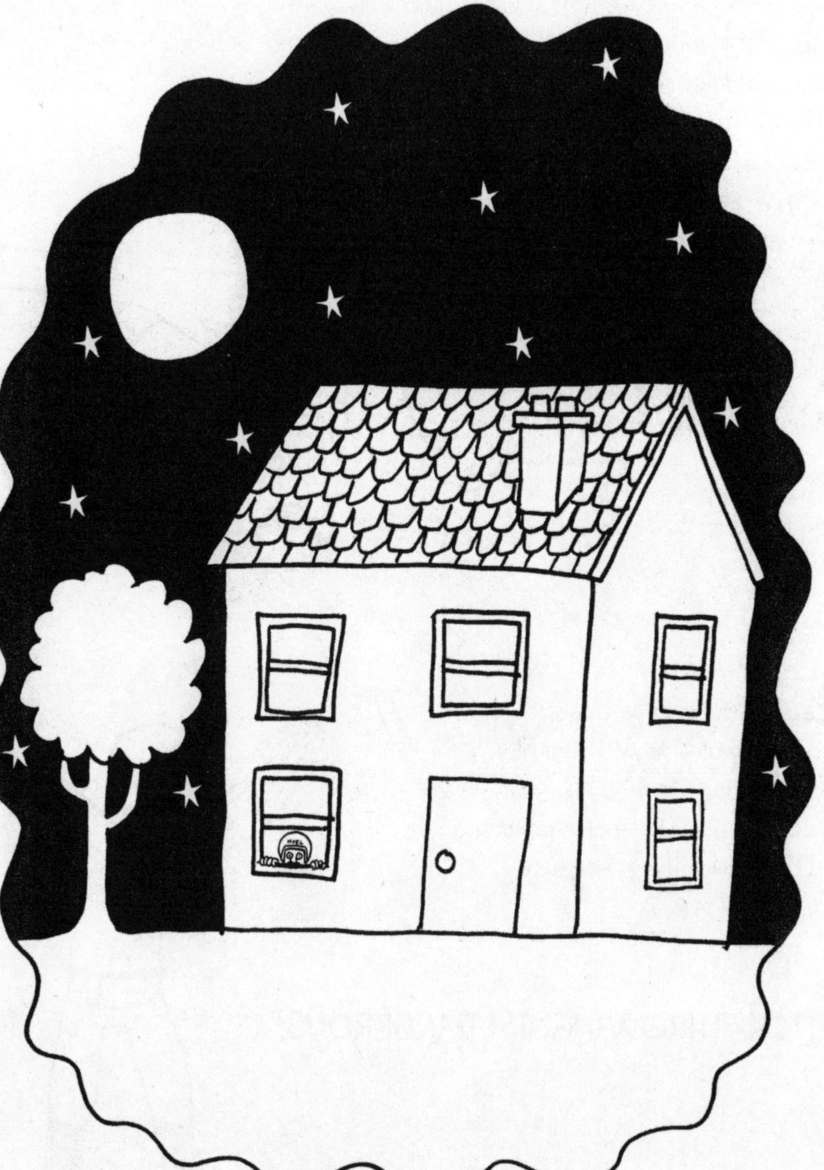

2. Werewolves, like all dogs, love to be patted and tickled. If you approach a werewolf confidently and pat it on the top of its head and tickle its tummy, it will roll onto its back, looking happy with its tongue out. If you do that to me, I will say, "Seriously, what on earth are you doing?"

Seriously . . .

3. If you throw a stick for a werewolf, it will happily fetch it and drop it at your feet. If you do that for me, I will be angry because

STICK THROWING IS DANGEROUS.

4. If you take a werewolf on a car journey with the window half down, it, like all dogs, will stick its head out and lick its chops as the wind blows its ears around.

I WILL NOT DO THAT.

I will sit still with my seat belt on and warn you if you are going too fast.

5. Finally, werewolves are **NOT** interested in

DANGER PREVENTION.

They do not worry about robot grannies or getting stuck underneath a cabbalanche.

They do not wear helmets.

A werewolf **IS THE OPPOSITE OF A DANGEROLOGIST.**

THEREFORE: I AM NOT A WEREWOLF.

Thank you.

POSTURE CHECK!

Make sure you are still sitting **UP STRAIGHT**
as discussed on page 2. Also check that

YOUR CHAIR IS STILL NOT ON FIRE

while you read this.

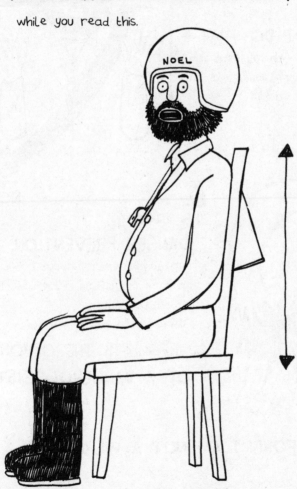

Now put on another pair of socks because we are about to tackle one of the things that

DANGEROLOGISTS FEAR THE MOST.

SNOW

It is hard to imagine a more dangerous thing than snow. Maybe if the ground was covered in marbles and you had a blindfold on. And there was a shark with wings flying around, swooping down from the trees. And it hadn't eaten for days. And you were wearing a coat made of sandwiches.

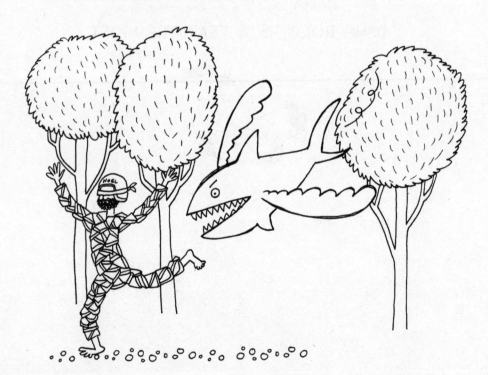

But at least then you could vacuum up the marbles. And telephone the flying-shark catcher or whoever you telephone when there's a flying shark. But with snow **THERE IS NOTHING YOU CAN DO, THERE IS NOBODY YOU CAN TELEPHONE.** Yes, you can shovel it away, **BUT MORE WILL TAKE ITS PLACE. SNOW IS TINY BLOBS OF PURE FROZEN DANGER.**

TTTFADIES

SNOW

1. The correct thing to do when it snows is to **SIB**. Just lie there with a large book and a pile of delicious cabbages, and wait until the snow melts.

2. But do people stay in bed? NO. They do the exact opposite of that. THEY GO OUTSIDE AND DO INCREDIBLY DANGEROUS THINGS!

Sledding!

Snowball fights!

Ice skating!

GOING OUTSIDE WITHOUT GLOVES ON! These are all things YOU MUST NOT EVER DO.

3. If you really insist on going outside, the first thing you need to do is **GET RID OF ALL THE SNOW.** This is easy to do in your yard by **LIGHTING TEN BARBECUES.**

Don't cook anything, though! **IT COULD CATCH ON FIRE!** Just wait for the snow to melt. If you manage to get rid of it all, congratulations. You have turned a **RAD** situation **NED.**

NOTE: This is the only use of barbecues I approve of.

4. **WAIT!** Before you do anything, you need to **GET DRESSED FOR SNOW.**

The normal **DANGER-ONESIE** is not warm enough for snow, so you must

wear a **FULL SNOWPROOF SNUGGLE-ONESIE.**

5. **A HELMET FLAG** will alert rescuers if you get stuck in a snow drift, and an

ALPINE HORN is essential in case you get lost in a blizzard.

NOTE: DO NOT USE A TRUMPET (see page 162).

6. The correct shoes for snow are **BED-SHOES**.

WHAT ARE BED-SHOES?

BED-SHOES are shoes made from beds. You can't move very fast in them **(GOOD)**, and their size makes it very hard to fall over. And if you do manage to fall over you will land **ON A SOFT BED**.

7. Having cleared your yard of all snow, it's time to get some **BALLS OF WHITE WOOL. WOOLBALL FIGHTS** are much less dangerous than snowball fights, and a woolball doesn't make you scream if it goes down the back of your neck.

8. Then gather together all the woolballs and build a

WOOLMAN. Give him a sprout (a fun-sized cabbage) for a nose and his own helmet. The great thing about a

WOOLMAN is that he won't melt, and if you really like him, you can knit him into a wool onesie that you can sleep in.

9. To go outside your yard into the snow

IS INCREDIBLY DANGEROUS.

What if your **BED-SHOES** get frozen solid and you are stuck?
The mean children from the school at the end of the road
certainly won't help. They'll just throw snowballs at you

and call you **ABOMNOEL SNOWMAN** if your name is Noel

(BASED ON ACTUAL EVENTS).

10. Another **HORRIBLE DANGER** is that you could trip on an object in your yard that has been covered by the snow. Three years ago I fell over Dennis and broke my arm. Now I make sure he stays in at night after his evening walk.

LOOK OUT FOR ANYTHING YOU'D FIND IN A YARD!

For example, a brush or a hose or a **GARDEN GNOME**.

GNOME + SNOW = RAD

REMEMBER: Always carry a pack of cards in case you get chased by a polar bear.

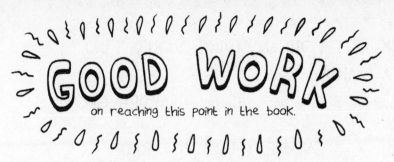

GOOD WORK

on reaching this point in the book.

With the **DETBAFOD** rapidly approaching, it is vital that you **REMAIN ALERT and in PEAK CONDITION.**
This might be a good time to get a snack, such as my second
favorite food after cabbages: **TOAST.**

TTTFADIES

HOW TO MAKE TOAST (WAFOS)

1. Toast-making must always begin with some **POWDMBing.**
Clear your entire yard (this doesn't take me very long).

EVERYTHING has to go. If you have a shed, it could
catch on fire, so get rid of it. Same with any trees and bushes.
They all have to go. When your entire yard is clear, cover
it with tin foil. You will need at least one hundred rolls.

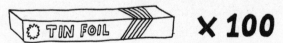

⚙ TIN FOIL   **X 100**

2. Place the toaster in the
center of this area.

3. Put on a fully fireproof suit complete with face mask and gloves. If you do not have a fireproof suit, an astronaut suit will do. If you don't have an astronaut suit, just wear an ordinary suit of armor.

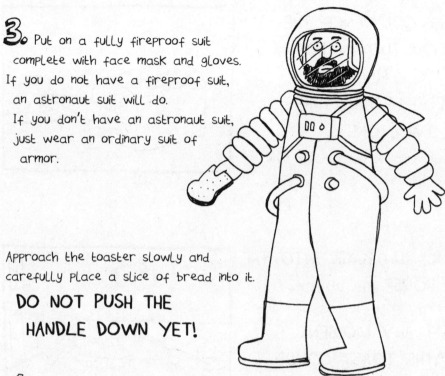

Approach the toaster slowly and carefully place a slice of bread into it.

DO NOT PUSH THE HANDLE DOWN YET!

4. Get ready to push the toaster handle down using a seesaw.

THIS IS THE ONLY USE OF A SEESAW I APPROVE OF!

But **DO NOT PUSH IT DOWN YET!**

First you have to do a countdown.

153

5. COMMENCE THE COUNTDOWN TO TOASTING:
FIVE, FOUR, THREE, TWO, ONE—

now seesaw the toaster **ON**.

6. RUN BACK INTO THE HOUSE. This is the most dangerous point in the operation. **AT ANY MOMENT THE TOAST COULD EXPLODE (TID).**

7. If the toast does not explode/burst into flames, it will pop up after about three minutes. **BUT DO NOT APPROACH IT YET!**

Wait for at least one hour.

8. When one hour has passed, and if a bird or giraffe hasn't stolen it, you may approach the toaster again, and pick up the toast with a long pair of safety tongs.

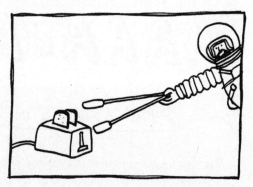

9. Leave to cool for another hour. Now your toast is ready to eat and is **RED**.

10. Remember to remove your spacesuit/armor before eating.

AAAAaAAA

SHARK ATTACKS IN THE HOME

Thankfully, shark attacks away from the ocean are rare. Occasionally a flood can lead to a shark getting into a basement or yard, but this doesn't happen very often and the shark is usually very easy to spot.

The real shark danger at home is being attacked by a shark **WHILE YOU ARE SITTING ON THE TOILET.**

HOW TO AVOID A TOILET-SHARK ATTACK

1. Never sit there for too long. The toilet shark is very indecisive and takes at least five minutes to make up its mind to do anything. So **DO YOUR BUSINESS AND GO, GO, GO.**

2. NEVER eat any food while sitting on the toilet, particularly **SANDWICHES.** Although the toilet shark will eat whatever it can get, its food of choice is **THE SANDWICH.**

3. TOILET SHARKS HATE JAZZ. If you are really worried about a toilet-shark attack, you should sing a jazz song to yourself. That will keep them away.

SHOOBY SHOOBY DO WEE BOP

4. ALWAYS SHUT THE TOILET SEAT WHEN YOU ARE DONE!

The toilet shark may try to leap from the toilet into the sink or bathtub. If you happen to be in the bathtub, this is really bad.

Then your only chance is to try to poke it with a toothbrush or, better still, poke it with

A TOOTHBRUSH SNAKE.

Sorry, I should definitely have reminded you about

TEPOC again before you read that one (see page 29).

I AM STILL SHAKING AFTER WRITING IT.

And I'm afraid that things are

NOT ABOUT TO GET ANY LESS FRIGHTENING.

MUSICAL DANGER

PLAYING AN INSTRUMENT

Playing music can be relaxing and fun. However, some instruments are a

WAKEY-WAKEY, BEEP-BEEP, TICK-TOCK ALARM CLOCK TO TERROR AND MAYHEM (WWBBTTACTTAM).

The most dangerous musical instruments are:

1. DRUMS

Drums, played badly, sound like a number of frightening things: thunder, a gorilla trying to escape from a caravan, some drums falling down a flight of stairs, or a large group of elephants stampeding.

The last one is **ESPECIALLY DANGEROUS** because, if you know anything about elephants, you will know that what makes elephants stampede **IS THE SOUND OF OTHER ELEPHANTS STAMPEDING.**

So **NEVER PLAY THE DRUMS CLOSE TO ELEPHANTS.**

In fact, hearing drums makes all animals stampede, so never play the drums close to any groups of animals. Some stampedes are more dangerous than others.

Stampeding tropical fish **(NED)**

Stampeding kittens **(GABMD)**

Stampeding elephants **(RAD)**

2. TRUMPET

Yes, the trumpet can be very useful for removing a toothbrush snake, but beware.

A badly played trumpet in mountainous areas can lead to **ROCK FALLS** in summer and **AVALANCHES** in winter.

A trumpet played near the coast can sound like a foghorn and may cause panic for ships at sea.

Most dangerous of all, the **PAAARP** of a trumpet can sound very like the **PAAAARP** of a vampire's fart and may **ATTRACT OTHER VAMPIRES**.

PAAARP

3. THE ACCORDION

This is the only instrument that **CAN ATTACK YOU.**
Heavy, stretchy, and sounding like a moany dinosaur, the accordion
lets you think you are in charge **UNTIL IT DECIDES TO**
TAKE OVER. Then you are stuck under it until somebody
comes to lift it off.

4. RECORDER/FLUTE/TIN WHISTLE

These whistly instruments are quieter than the rest, but no less
dangerous. Their high pitch can sound like a bird in trouble,
and this may summon a search party of other members of the
bird's family. This is cute if the bird is a sparrow, or even a
friendly owl, **BUT NOT CUTE AT ALL IF IT IS**
AN OSTRICH OR AN EMU.

5. THE PIANO WALRUS

Getting its name from its distinctive shape and black and white teeth, the piano walrus can easily be confused for a grand piano that has washed up on a beach.

WARNING: Never try to play a piano walrus!

It is not a piano, **IT IS A WALRUS**. Don't even approach it. The piano walrus is a very grumpy animal. If it wakes up, startled by somebody poking its teeth, it will be **VERY** unhappy.

This is why many famous pianists always carry a **STINKY FISH** in their top pocket. Often they will dangle it over a piano they haven't played before. Once they are certain that it's not a walrus, they will begin their concert.

SOME SAFE MUSICAL INSTRUMENTS

1. THE VIOLIN

With all of its strings, the violin makes
an awful sound. Like an old cat in
the rain. But if you remove all of the
strings it makes no sound at all.
So you can hum your
favorite song as you
silently swish away.

2. THE TUBA

Like the trumpet, the tuba sounds
terrible when you blow into it.
So why not fill it with dirt,
leave it out in your yard,
and grow a plant in it.
That's much more relaxing than
listening to it.

3. THE CABBAGE

Some people may try to tell you that the cabbage isn't a musical instrument. Don't listen to these people. Instead, listen to the beautiful sound a cabbage makes when you hit it with a wooden spoon.

Now get a slightly smaller cabbage and hit that.

THAT'S RIGHT! A slightly different thump sound.

Now line up eight of them to make yourself a

CABBAGE-O-PHONE and play all of your favorite

cabbage songs such as:

★ "Old McCabbage Had a Cabbage"

  ★ "We Wish You a Merry Cabbage (And a Sprouty New Year)"

   ★ Samuel Barber's "Cabbagio for Strings"

DOCTER NOEL'S ~ Relaxing ~ FAIRY ~ TALES

(WAFOS)

You have made it this far through this book and nothing really bad has happened to you, so **WELL DONE ON THAT.** As a reward, here is another classic fairy tale, slightly rewritten by me.

The Three Little Pigs

Once upon a time, three little pigs lived in a forest. They lived in a forest because they had escaped from their farm after an argument with the farmer over whether they should be turned into sausages.
He had been in favor of the idea.
They had been strongly against it.

In the end, they decided to escape from the farm by posing as recyclable goods.

Once in the forest, they quickly realized that it is quite
cold in forests. Also, there are hairy spiders, and a squirrel
told them about a rumor of a wolf.

They thought about going back to the farm, but then remembered
about the sausages. So they decided to stay in the forest
and built some accommodation.

Luckily one of the pigs knew quite a lot about building and construction (there had been building work on the farm when he lived there, and he was very nosy).

PIGGY HOUSE PLANS

So he set about building houses from the newest and strongest materials, complete with burglar alarms and security cameras.

They heard a rumor afterward that the wolf had arrived one night and had tried to get in by blowing, which is a very strange way to try to get into a house. He didn't have a chance. I mean, who has ever tried to get into a house by blowing?

Maybe if he had been a whale he might have been able to knock the door in by blowing water through his spout,

BUT WHAT WOULD A WHALE BE DOING IN A FOREST?

Anyway, the houses stood for another ten years and the pigs
were very happy, until one day a volcano erupted nearby
and the whole forest and neighboring farms
(including that of the farmer) got covered in lava and
the pigs ended up getting cooked anyway.

MORAL: DON'T BUILD YOUR HOME NEAR A VOLCANO

because

DANGER IS EVERYWHERE

DOCTER NOEL'S GUIDE TO DANCING

With all of this **INCREDIBLY IMPORTANT AND SERIOUS DANGEROLOGY**, you are probably wondering how I relax. What does Docter Noel Zone do to chill out and get away from it all?

This may surprise you, but I love to dance. Everyone is born with one talent, but I seem to have two:

DANGEROLOGY

and **DANCING**.

1. BREAK DANCING

As you will realize, if you have paid any attention to this book so far, normal break dancing is **MUCH, MUCH** too dangerous.

ALL that leaping and spinning around, with your arms and legs going everywhere,

IT IS BASICALLY KARATE WITHOUT THE SUIT ON.

However, I have invented some new break dancing moves that are perfectly safe.

THE TOASTER

We all know The Robot, **BUT WHAT IF A REAL ROBOT SEES YOU DOING IT AND TAKES YOU BACK TO THEIR ROBOT PLANET?** No, a much safer version of The Robot is **THE TOASTER. THE TOASTER** captures all the excitement of waiting for my second favorite food to be ready.

HOW TO DO THE TOASTER

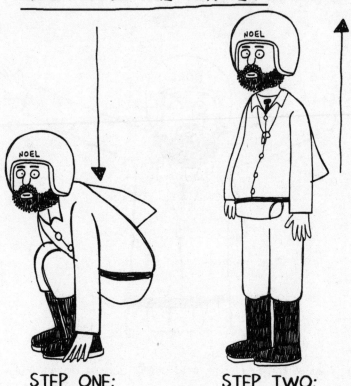

STEP ONE:
Crouch down.

STEP TWO:
Three minutes later, POP UP.

THE SLEEPY KITTEN

You may be familiar with The Worm—another break-dancing move that involves throwing yourself around on the ground.

Well, this is what I have to say about The Worm: **TID!**

I have picked a much less dangerous animal to base my moves on: **THE SLEEPY KITTEN.**

HOW TO DO THE SLEEPY KITTEN

STEP ONE:
Lie down on the ground.

STEP TWO:

Don't move, but occasionally go "meow meow meow,"
like you are a cat having a cat dream.

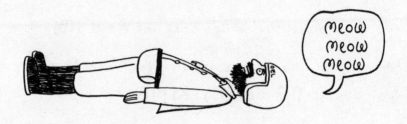

STEP THREE: That's it.

Similar to The Sleepy Kitten is a move inspired by Dennis:

THE STONE

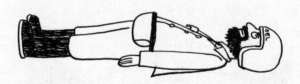

It is the same as The Sleepy Kitten, but without any meowing.

2. BALLET

I always cry when I see ballet. Not at the beauty of the dance **BUT AT THE DANGER. WHY IS EVERYONE RUNNING AROUND ON THEIR TIPPY TOES?** If somebody trips up, **YOU WILL ALL FALL DOWN LIKE BIG FRILLY DOMINOES.**

Here are some 100% safe ballets you can perform on your own.

SWAN PARKING LOT

Similar to the famous *Swan Lake*, except where the
swan is waddling around the parking lot beside the lake.
It occasionally eats some bread, and it occasionally makes
very loud quacking sounds at ducks and cars.

THE NUTCRACKER 2

In *The Nutcracker 2*, the sequel to
The Nutcracker, the nuts have all been
cracked open. So you can just sit in your
tutu at the table and eat them.

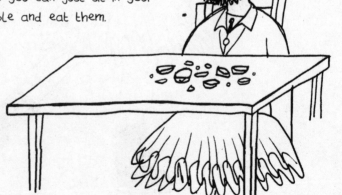

3. BALLROOM DANCING

The main danger here is that you could throw your partner somewhere. Maybe out a window, or up high, on top of something.

The key to making it safer is to make the music calmer. Instead of rock and roll or big-band music, choose something else. How about getting rid of music and performing to a background of a weather forecast or a radio documentary on the history of socks?

And, instead of a partner, why not use a cabbage?

The great thing about dancing with a cabbage is that you can imagine it is anyone.

Even the person who sold you the cabbage in her shop.

AAAAaAAA

GHOSTS

(OK, OK, I realize that ghosts aren't animals, so this should be **AAAAaAGA.**)

The first thing to know about ghosts is that what people think are ghosts

ARE NEVER GHOSTS.
They are creaky pipes
or the wind blowing through
cracks or a mean big brother
with a flashlight and a sheet, making ghost noises.

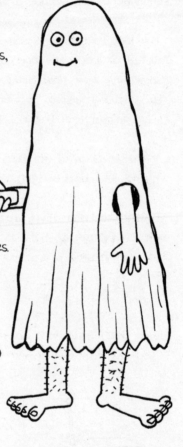

The second thing most people don't know about ghosts is that they are

INCREDIBLY BORING.
I know some people (Katherine and Millicent)
think that I am incredibly boring.
Well, imagine how boring you would have
to be for me to describe you
as incredibly boring.

The other important thing about ghosts is that

GHOSTS ARE REALLY SCARED OF EVERYTHING.
Loud noises, someone jumping out at them, wasps.

But the thing that really **PETRIFIES** ghosts most of all is:

BUBBLES

Just a single one, blown in their direction, will cause any ghost to scream and run off in the opposite direction and never come back.

So, if you are ever worried about a ghost, take your bubbles out of your **PEBB** and get ready to turn a **WOOOOO** into a **NOOOOOOO**.

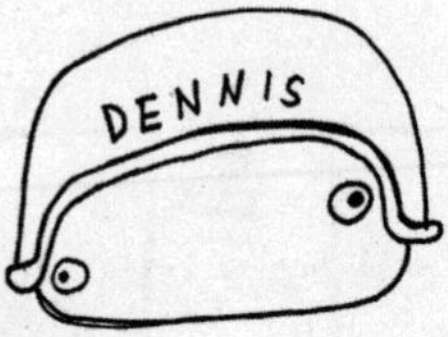
DENNIS

With the **DETBAFOD** fast approaching,
I'm afraid we still have some really, awfully
dangerous sections still to get through.

Beginning with the night of the year

every **FOD** fears . . .

HALLOWEEN

It's like **SOMEBODY TRIED TO THINK OF A NIGHT THAT WOULD ANNOY ME THE MOST.**

People disguising themselves and going around in the dark trying to scare each other?
Making their houses look haunted with skulls and bats and scary lights?

CUTTING UP PUMPKINS WITH SHARP KNIVES AND THEN PUTTING FIRE INSIDE THEM?

NO! NO! TID! RAD!

But, for some reason, my nieces Katherine and Millicent love it. So this year I tried to show them how to have a safe and fun Halloween, **WAFOS.**

1. COSTUMES

I am not against the idea of dressing up. It's just that many costumes are **VERY DANGEROUS IN EMERGENCY SITUATIONS.**

Imagine if you were dressed up as a pirate and **A GROUP OF ACTUAL PIRATES SAW YOU AND CHALLENGED YOU TO A SWORDFIGHT?**

TID!

Imagine if a Lion had escaped from the zoo

AND YOU WERE DRESSED IN A ZEBRA COSTUME!

RAD!

Also why do so many Halloween costumes try to be so scary?
With a little bit of imagination, they can be safe and fun.

2. SAFE FANCY-DRESS OPTIONS

Mini Docter Noel Zone costume: See my fashion dos and don'ts section on page 121 to get the full look.

Then go to houses, reading sections from this book.

Yourself, yesterday: This costume involves wearing whatever you were wearing yesterday.

Yourself, tomorrow, also known as **ME IN THE FUTURE:** This costume involves wearing the clothes you are wearing now, again tomorrow.

Yourself, tonight: This costume involves putting on your pajamas and going to bed early. It is the safest costume of all.

Here are the costumes I created for Millicent and Katherine.

Millicent is dressed up as a cabbage.
I made this using thirty-five cabbages from

GRETEL'S CABBAGE CABIN.
Underneath all those leaves
I'm sure she's very happy!

The other great thing about
this costume is that afterward
I can boil up the cabbages to
make cabbage soup to give to
people who come trick-or-treating!

I have dressed Katherine up
as the greatest pet of all:

THE STONE. I have done
this by attaching lots of
stones to her.

Unfortunately this makes her
costume too heavy to walk
around in, so I had to wheel
her around in a wheelbarrow.

TRICK-OR-TREATING

It is **MUCH TOO DANGEROUS** to walk around,
going to houses in the dark, so I took the girls out
first thing in the morning. Nobody was awake yet,
which is good because nobody answers their door,

so **NO UNHEALTHY TREATS.**

For trick-or-treaters who come to

THE DANGERZONE, in addition to
cabbage soup, every year
I hand out a pamphlet I have written
on safety at Halloween. But, to be honest,
nobody comes to my house anymore.

Gretel gets a lot more trick-or-treaters than I do. She must give
out something even more delicious than cabbage soup.

Last year, while I was standing in my yard waiting for my first trick-or-treaters, I noticed that she had one much older trick-or-treater, who had come dressed as a policewoman.

I could hear Gretel talking about her gnome (Mr. Chomsky), who had gone missing. Gretel was explaining what Mr. Chomsky looks like to her visitor, who I soon realized was not looking for candy but was an actual policewoman.

Mr. Chomsky

She told Gretel that there's very little the police can do about gnome-napping. And it might have been the local kids that took him for a prank, and they could put him back soon.

Gretel sounded sad, and I felt like climbing over the fence to talk to her. But then I remembered that it was the same policewoman from the pond/crocodile incident who had told me that I can't climb into neighbors' yards without their permission.

Gretel is much prettier than this.

NOEL

POOR GRETEL.

Everyone needs a break once in a while, but remember:

THERE IS NEVER A VACATION FROM DANGER.

TTTFADIES

GOING ON VACATION

1. Don't go very far! My rhymes will help you to remember the two golden rules:

The farther you've gone,
The more things can go wrong

and

Pack a medium-sized lunchbox
full of sandwiches

And come back when you've finished
all the sandwiches.

(That one doesn't rhyme as nicely.)

2. Camping vacations are fun. But why not park the camper outside your own house? Why not camp in your yard? Or if you don't have a yard, why not pitch the tent in your living room? That way you don't have far to go to get more sandwiches.

3. Boat vacations are an idea, but rivers and canals are **SO DANGEROUS**. Why not put the boat on a trailer and park it outside your house?

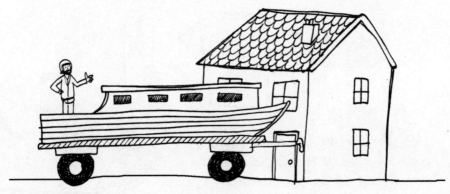

4. Terrible things can happen on cruise-ship vacations. **WHAT ABOUT PIRATES? WHAT ABOUT SHARKS?** What if the ship sinks and you have to swim to a desert island **AND YOU HATE COCONUTS**? No way.

You Cruise, You Lose.

5. When visiting the seaside, remember the basics: sunblock, a hat, a T-shirt to cover up, and plenty of water to drink.

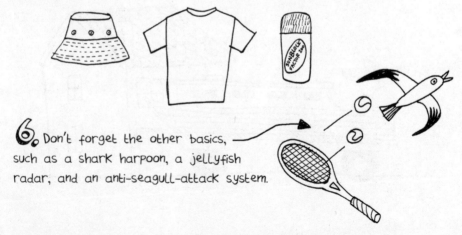

6. Don't forget the other basics, such as a shark harpoon, a jellyfish radar, and an anti-seagull-attack system.

7. A fishing vacation is relaxing.

UNTIL YOU CATCH SOMETHING.

What if you caught a shark? Or an octopus?
Or an octoshark (an octopus holding eight sharks)?
Make sure you never catch anything by not having a
hook on the end of your fishing line. And beware of waves.
Best just to sit in your car and imagine you are fishing.

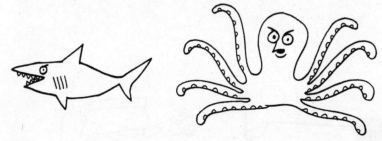

8. A SAFARI? **A SAFARI!** As if life wasn't dangerous
enough already. Why not go on vacation to a wasps' nest

OR STAY WITH A FAMILY OF RATTLESNAKES?

HOTEL WASP

9. EXTREME SPORTS HOLIDAY?

White-water rafting? Kitesurfing? **Bungee jumping?**

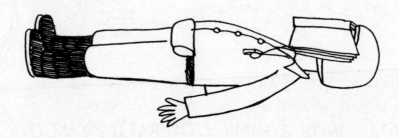

(Sorry, I had to lie down with the book open on **TEPOC** over my face to recover from just writing those words.)

10. Instead of going on vacation, why not stay at home and

PRETEND YOU'VE GONE ON VACATION?

Turn the heat up and put bananas everywhere to create a
tropical island. Leave the freezer open and put on your
snuggle-onesie to simulate a ski trip.

Send a postcard to Gretel with "Wish you were here!"
on the front, like you always do, but this time don't
leave it blank so she has no idea who it came from.

SIGN YOUR NAME.

STAY STRONG, PODs!

Keep concentrating and memorizing!

The **DETBAFOD** is getting closer all the time.

Just think how good it will feel to sign your name on that **DOD**!

It will not feel good to read this next section, though, because it is

REALLY REALLY TERRIFYING.

AAAAaAAA

THE MAILBOX OCTOPUS

We all love to get a letter or card in the mail, but people don't send as many as they used to. Some put this down to the rise of e-mail and texting, but I put it down to another thing;

THE MAILBOX OCTOPUS.

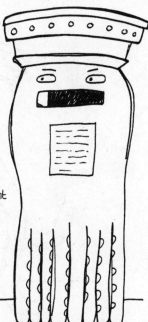

THE MAILBOX OCTOPUS
(or MAILBOCTOPUS) is a rare and mysterious kind of octopus that occasionally appears on street corners. How they get there, nobody knows for sure, but it is thought THEY SQUEEZE THEMSELVES UP THROUGH DRAINS.

Once they've found a spot,

THEY TAKE ON THE APPEARANCE OF A MAILBOX—

green in some countries, red or blue in others—and they open their
large, rectangular mouths.

Then they wait.

They wait for you to come along to mail your letter.
And, when your hand pushes the letter into the slot,

IT GRABS YOU.

By the time you realize what is going on, it has wrapped you
up with two of its tentacles and is marching you off down
the street with the other six, toward the sea and its octopus lair.

WHAT TO DO IF YOU'VE BEEN GRABBED BY A MAILBOX OCTOPUS

Having so many long arms is the main strength of the mailbox octopus, **BUT IT IS ALSO ITS WEAKNESS.**

It is also incredibly ticklish. You can kick and shout all you want and nothing will happen, but one carefully placed tickle and the octopus will drop you and collapse into a giggling mess.

Ticklish spot X 8

Giving you time to run off down the street, shouting

"THAT'S NOT A MAILBOX. IT'S AN OCTOPUS!"

Soon, somebody from the nearest post office will come and load the mailboctopus into a sack. Then it will be sent **VERY** far out to sea, far from a town where it might try that trick again. Oh, and you're going to have to write that letter again. It is gone.

DON'T GIVE UP NOW!

You are nearly there!

Soon you will have your own **T-COD**
fluttering in the breeze behind you, a fully
qualified **DANGEROLOGIST** (Level 1).

You just have to make it
through the next few sections!

EVERYDAY DANGER PREVENTION

AT THE PLAYGROUND IN THE PARK

So many dangerous things can happen on a trip to the park.
You can be:

1. Eaten by a killer whale while you're trying to feed the ducks.

2. Kidnapped by swans while you're trying to feed the ducks.

3. Chopped in half by a Frisbee.

But the most dangerous part of the park is definitely

THE PLAYGROUND.

I don't think they should be called playgrounds.

I think they should be called **ACCIDENT MAGNETS.**

There are so many awful things to **POWDMB** to

all **PWINAPODs.**

Oh, a seesaw is fun, going up and down, is it?

WELL, WHAT HAPPENS IF A VERY LARGE PERSON SITS ON ONE END?

I'll tell you what happens, **SOMETHING RAD:** It turns

INTO A HUMAN CATAPULT.

Oh, **THE SWINGS** are safe? Well, what happens when somebody pushes you too hard?

IT TURNS INTO A HUMAN CATAPULT!

What about a merry-go-round?

WHAT HAPPENS WHEN IT GOES TOO FAST?
IT TURNS INTO A . . . you get the message.

But with a little imagination, playgrounds can be used for important non-dangerous activities.

THE MERRY-GO-ROUND

Merry-go-rounds make you dizzy and sick. However, they are an excellent way to dry a wet dog.

THE SLIDE

An excellent alternative use for the slide is as

A HOT-LIQUID COOLER.

Is your soup or tea or coffee too hot to drink? Simply pour it down the slide, and by the time you catch it again at the bottom, it will be cool enough to drink. Leftover bits of soup also stop children from sliding on it in the future.

NOBODY WANTS SOUPY LEGS.

SWINGS make excellent hanging baskets for plants,

and **JUNGLE GYMS** are the perfect place to hang damp clothes.

Finally, place bricks under each end of the seesaw and you
have transformed it into a **SEATSAW**, where people can sit
and drink their not-too-hot soup, or wait for their
dogs or clothes to dry.

Or think about the posters that Gretel has put on lamp posts
and trees in the area asking if anyone has seen her gnome.

Oh, Gretel.

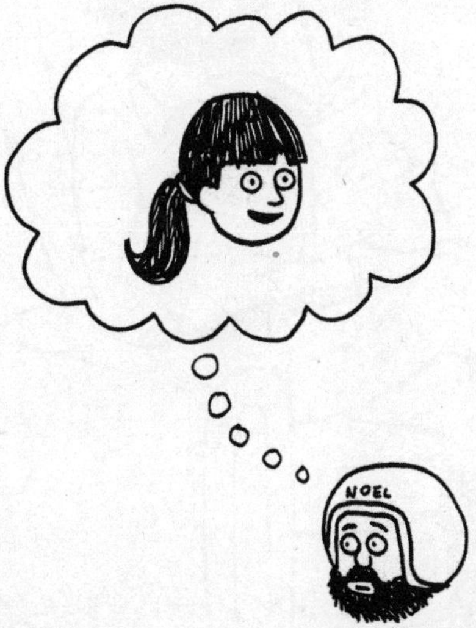
NOEL

DOCTER NOEL'S ~Relaxing~ FAIRY ~ TALES

(WAFOS)

Here is the final installment of my non-dangerous fairy-tale series and, let me warn you, **THIS IS BY FAR THE MOST HORRIFYING.**

GOLDILOCKS
AND THE
THREE BEARS

One day Goldilocks's soccer ball bounced into the front yard of a house at the end of her road. As she ran in to pick it up, she noticed a sign on the front door that said **THE THREE BEARS**. No way, she thought to herself. Bears don't live in houses. They live in caves or woods or on television. Or close to where you find honey. It must just be an unusual name, like Goldilocks Five-Goats, her full name.

°THE THREE° BEARS

Then she noticed some huge footprints across the grass and on the path. They were very big and seemed to have claws. Maybe they just have a big dog, Goldilocks Five-Goats thought to herself. From inside the house, Goldilocks heard a sound a lot like a bear.

"RAAAAARRRRRRR."

Yes, it must be a really big dog, she said to herself. Then a delivery scooter pulled up and a man jumped off. "Are you one of The Three Bears? Did you order pizzas covered in honey?"

As the front door opened behind her, Goldilocks heard a roar that definitely did not belong to any kind of dog. She sprinted past the delivery man and was safely back in the Five-Goats home ten seconds later.

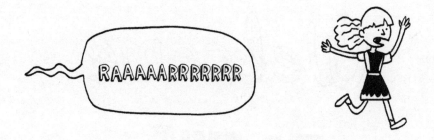

RAAAAARRRRRR

Just as well. That evening the bears dined on their favorite meal of all: delivery man with a side order of honey pizza.

MORAL: BEARS! AAAAAGH! TIABA!

Welcome

TO THE

DANGERZONE

(PART 2)

YOU ARE NEARLY THERE!

As a treat before the **DETBAFOD**—now that we really know each other—Dennis and I would like to invite you

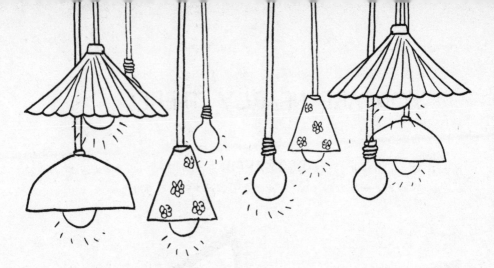

To make sure we don't trip over things, I keep

VERY BRIGHT LIGHTS ON ALL THE TIME.

They are so bright Dennis and I need to wear sunglasses when we are inside. Which you could say cancels out the point of the bright lights in the first place, but I think makes us look **PRETTY COOL.**

I like paintings on the walls, but if the pictures are **TOO REALISTIC** somebody might confuse them for **AN OPEN WINDOW** and try to stick their head out.

TID! TID!

To prevent this I add **A UNICORN** to each picture, as **I KNOW FOR SURE THAT THERE ARE NO UNICORNS IN MY YARD.**

I also write across all the pictures **"THIS IS NOT A WINDOW"** to be extra safe.

We will begin on the ground floor. In fact, that's the only part we can go to as I REMOVED THE STAIRS SOME TIME AGO. Sure, it means you can't go up, BUT IT ALSO MEANS THAT YOU CAN'T FALL DOWN.

I don't believe in shelves **(THEY CAN FALL DOWN, TOO),**
so I keep everything on the floor.

This makes the floor pretty cluttered.

MY BEDROOM

A common mistake is to think that danger is finished once you get into bed. You've done everything you had to do, and now you can lie back and relax, safe in the knowledge that nothing else can go wrong.

YOU ARE ALMOST A FOD (Level 1)! You can't think like this any more.

DANGER IS AT ITS MOST DANGEROUS WHEN YOU LEAST EXPECT IT.

Just because you're lying down doesn't mean you can't fall over. **YOUR BED COULD COLLAPSE** or, worse, you could fall out of it, perhaps on to your pet stone

(OWWW FOR BOTH OF YOU).

The ideal bed is not shaped like a bed. It is much closer to the ground and has hard sides so you can't fall out. Ideally it is also waterproof and shaped like a boat so you can float off in the event of a flood/volcano.

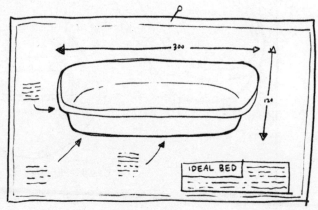

CORRECT! THE IDEAL BED IS A BATHTUB.

I have been sleeping in a bathtub for over ten years.

You get used to the hardness after about five years,

AND YOU DON'T HAVE FAR TO GO TO BRUSH YOUR TEETH IN THE MORNING.

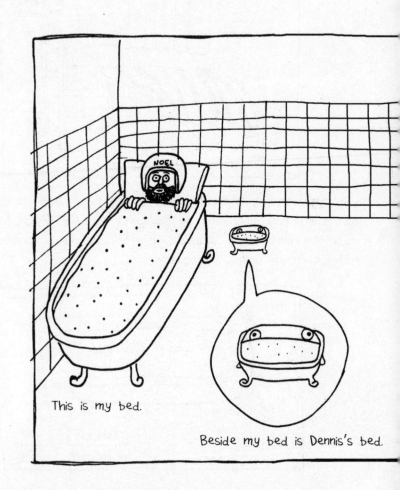

This is my bed.

Beside my bed is Dennis's bed.

Beside that is the toilet.

Oh.

OK,
I ADMIT IT!
I DID TAKE GRETEL'S GNOME!

But I took him because the weather forecast said it
was going to snow!

SHE MIGHT HAVE FALLEN OVER HIM AND BROKEN
HER ARM, like I did!

I was going to put him back after the winter, but the policewoman
said I'm not allowed to go into my neighbors' yards anymore!

Oh, Gretel, I didn't know what to do!
But I've been looking after him very well.

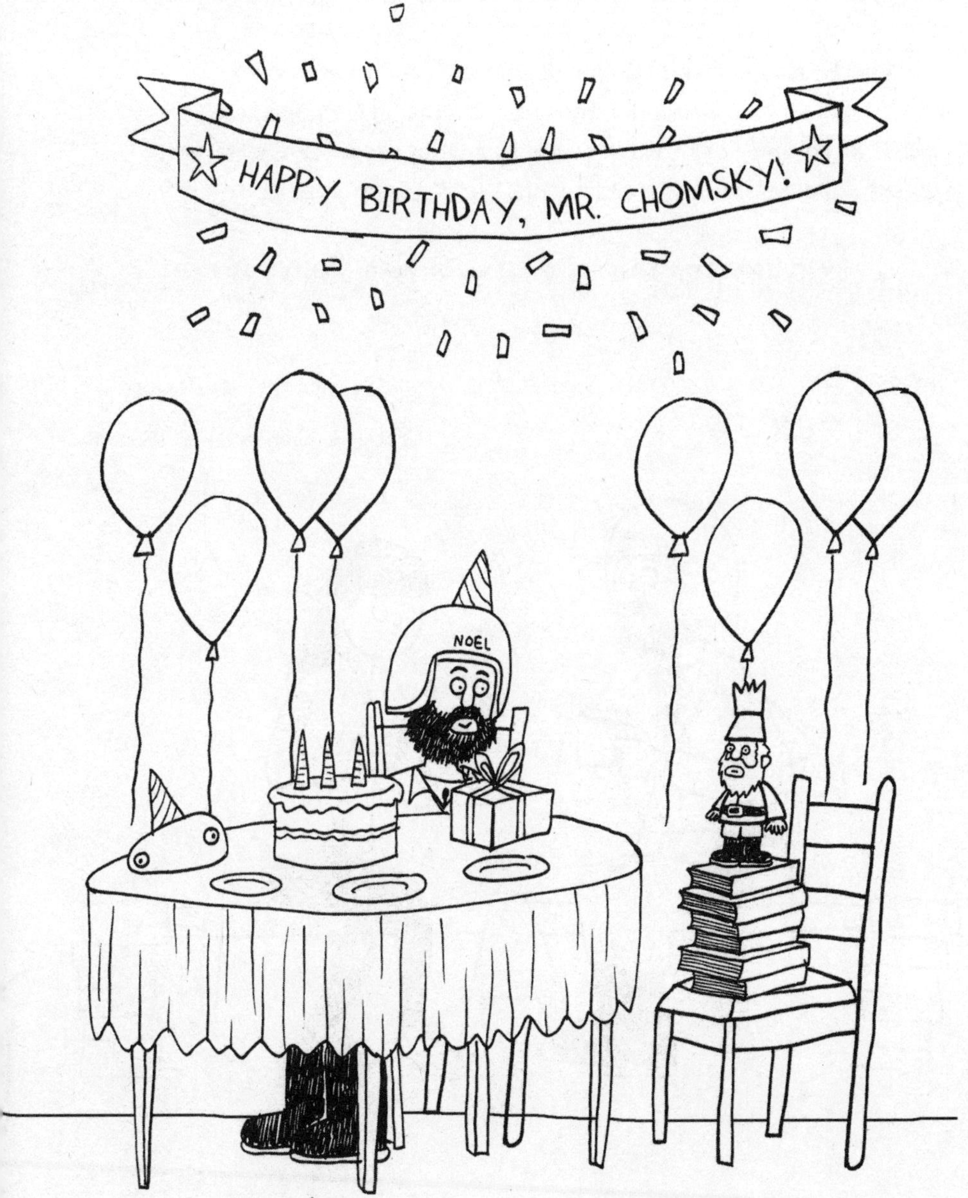
HAPPY BIRTHDAY, MR. CHOMSKY!
NOEL

So, if you ever read this, please come over and I'll give him back to you.

Then perhaps we could go for a cup of tea or coffee?
Well, those drinks would be too hot for me, but maybe we
could go to the park and I could pour mine down the slide and
afterward sit on the seatsaw and drink them.

I've never done this before, but I've written you a poem.

Gretel is even prettier than this.

228

Oh, Gretel. I've never said hello,
But I've wanted to for ages,
Living in the house next door
And buying your cabbages.

I wish that I was brave enough
To come over to your home.
I'd tell you that I think you're great
And sorry about the gnome.

Thank you.
(Sorry, Gretel.)

YOU'VE
MADE IT!

Now put on your chair-pants and your
  stationery sombrero because it's time for

YOUR DETBAFOD.

Note: If you don't own this book, **YOU CAN'T JUST
WRITE IN SOMEBODY ELSE'S COPY.**
So go to lb-kids.com to print out your own **DETBAFOD**
and **DOD.**

GOOD LUCK, POD!

DOCTER NOEL ZONE

~Presents~

Dangerology Examination To Become A Full-On Dangerologist

- There are ten questions.

- Write your answer neatly underneath each question, or check the box.

- You will find the correct answers at the end——**NO CHEATING.**

- **NOTE:** Remember to remove the safety sprout from the dangerous end of your pen/pencil.

1. You are walking home from school and a **PANTHER** is blocking your path. What do you do?

(a) Try to run away. ☑

(b) Reach into your **PEBB**, pull out your bubbles, and start blowing. ☐

(c) Shout **"TIAPA"** and start dancing. ☐

2. You are at the beach and a big wave washes up a grand piano. What do you do?

(a) Rush over ~~and start to play your favorite tune.~~ ☑

(b) Do not go near it. ☐

(c) Try to start a beach bonfire. ☐

3. Why should you never wear a green helmet with a brown onesie?

_____

_____

_____

4. Which of these songs is the best to play to remove a **TOOTHBRUSH SNAKE**?

(a) "Love Is All Around" ☐

(b) "I Will Always Love You" ☐

(c) "Baa, Baa, Black Sheep" ☑

5. Estimate how long it takes to make a slice of toast **SAFELY**.

(a) 3 minutes ☑

(b) 10 minutes ☐

(c) At least 3 hours ☑

6. Place these items in order of their **DANGER,** from **MOST DANGEROUS to NOT DANGEROUS AT ALL.**

Cabbage ☐

Swings in the park ☐

Bicycle ☐

7. How do you say "Hello, my name is Docter Noel Zone" to a pirate?

(a) "Yarrr, arrr arrr arrr Docter Noel Zone." ☑

(b) "Arrr, arrr yarrr arrr Docter Noel Zone." ☐

(c) "Yarrr, yarrr yarrr yarrr Docter Noel Zone." ☐

8. Why is there no need to buy your **DAD** a birthday present?

_____

_____

_____

9. Which is the best **SPLOD** that describes a cabbage?

(a) NAAD ☑

(b) ANDAAP, ANDAAO, and RED ☐

(c) RAD ☐

10. Which of these is the best number of people to invite to a birthday party?

(a) 50 ☐

(b) 17 ☐

(c) 1. And that person is Gretel. ☑

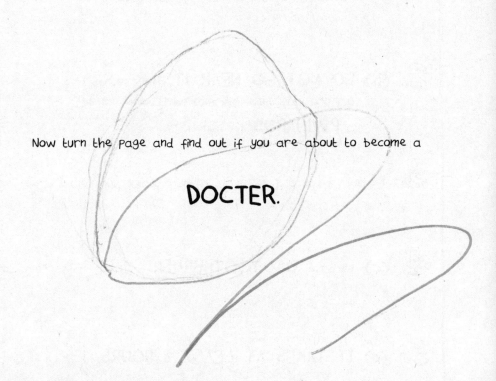

Now turn the page and find out if you are about to become a

DOCTER.

ANSWERS TO THE DANGEROLOGY EXAMINATION

1. (c) is the correct answer. You shout **"TIAPA"** ("This Is A Panther Alert") and start dancing. This would be a perfect time to perform *Swan Parking Lot*.

2. (b) **DO NOT GO NEAR IT.** That sounds like a piano walrus and it may well want to eat a **PWINAPOD** for dinner.

3. Because birds and squirrels might mistake you for a tree.

4. (c) because **THE TOOTHBRUSH SNAKE** hates love songs.

5. (c) **IT TAKES AT LEAST 3 HOURS.**

6. Most dangerous: **BICYCLE.**

Still very dangerous: **SWINGS.**

Not at all dangerous, but an excellent pet: **CABBAGE.**

7. (a) **THIS COULD SAVE YOUR SCHOOL TRIP.**

8. Because your **DAD** is a whistle that you wear around your neck.

9. (b) Cabbages are delicious and absolutely not dangerous, and they are also excellent pets.

10. (c) This would be the best birthday party ever.

If you didn't get all ten questions right, I'm afraid you have to go back to page 1 and **START THIS BOOK ALL OVER AGAIN.** If you got all ten right, then you can turn the page.

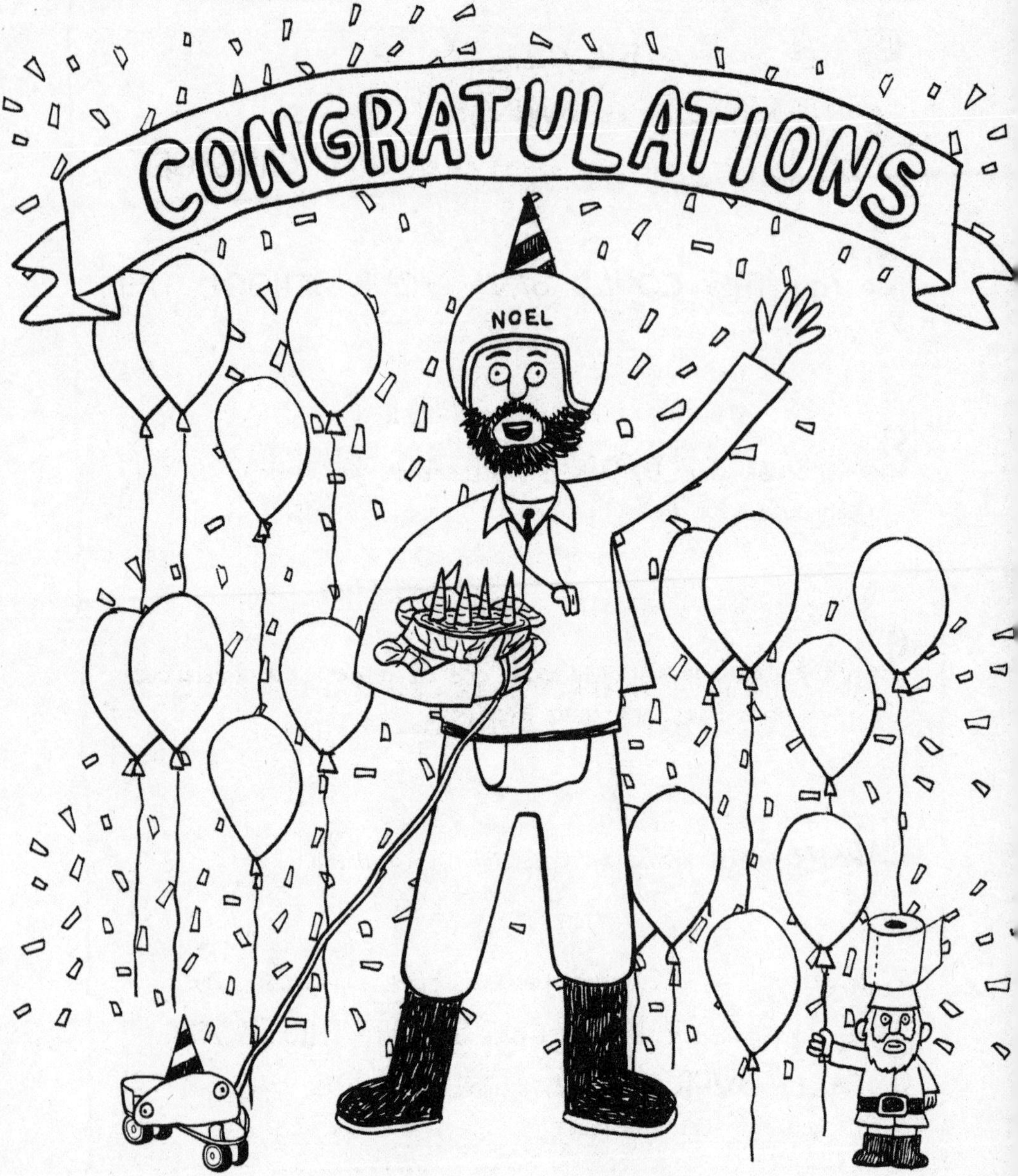
CONGRATULATIONS
NOEL

DOD (DIPLOMA OF DANGEROLOGY) Level 1

THIS IS TO CERTIFY THAT

DOCTER . . . .

(sign your name here)

has reached an excellent level of knowledge in

AAAAaAAA, TTTFADIES and **GENERAL DANGEROLOGY**

and is no longer a **PWINAPOD** or a **POD**, but now a **FOD** (Level 1).

You can now rightfully wear your own **T-COD.**

Good luck **LOFDing, POWDMBing** and **MSTDIDWEEIPSTIAing**

and remember at all times that

DANGER IS EVERYWHERE

**D N Z
CABBAGE
OF
APPROVAL**

Docter Noel Zone

DOCTER NOEL ZONE   (Level 5)

Thank you.

Ready for more DANGEROLOGY Lessons from Dr. Noel Zone?

DON'T MISS THE THIRD BOOK IN THE

DANGER IS EVERYWHERE SERIES!

Available June 2017

Turn the page (carefully!) for a sneak preview.

OK, so I don't know much about being a chef.

But I know **A HUGE AMOUNT** about **DANGER**. So, before
I begin this job tomorrow morning, here are my

TTTFADIES

(Top Ten Tips For Avoiding Danger In Everyday Situations)

in one of the most **DANGEROUS** places of all:

DANGER
AT
SCHOOL

1. RUSHING AROUND

The most common cause of **ACCIDENTS** at school is people **RUSHING AROUND THE PLACE**. Eliminate this risk by insisting that everyone wears **VERY SLOW FOOTWEAR**. For example, **SNOWSHOES, HAY BALES,** or **VELCRO SOLES.**

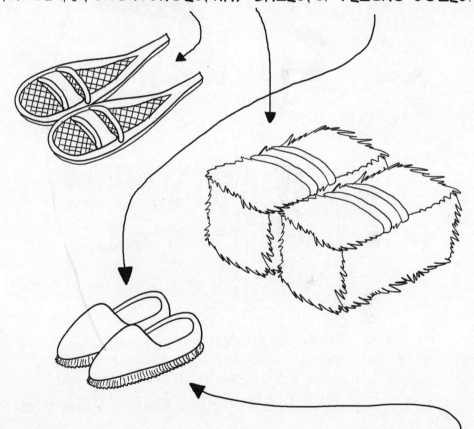

NOTE: This one only works if you have hairy school carpets.

2. SCHOOL UNIFORMS

AWFUL SCHOOL UNIFORM DANGERS are waiting to happen every day.

Instead, all students should wear protective headwear, along with sturdy boots, a full-length onesie, and why not finish off the look with a handy (and stylish) **PEBB** (**P**ersonal **E**mergency **B**um **B**ag)?

 NOTE: Correct. Everyone should dress like me.

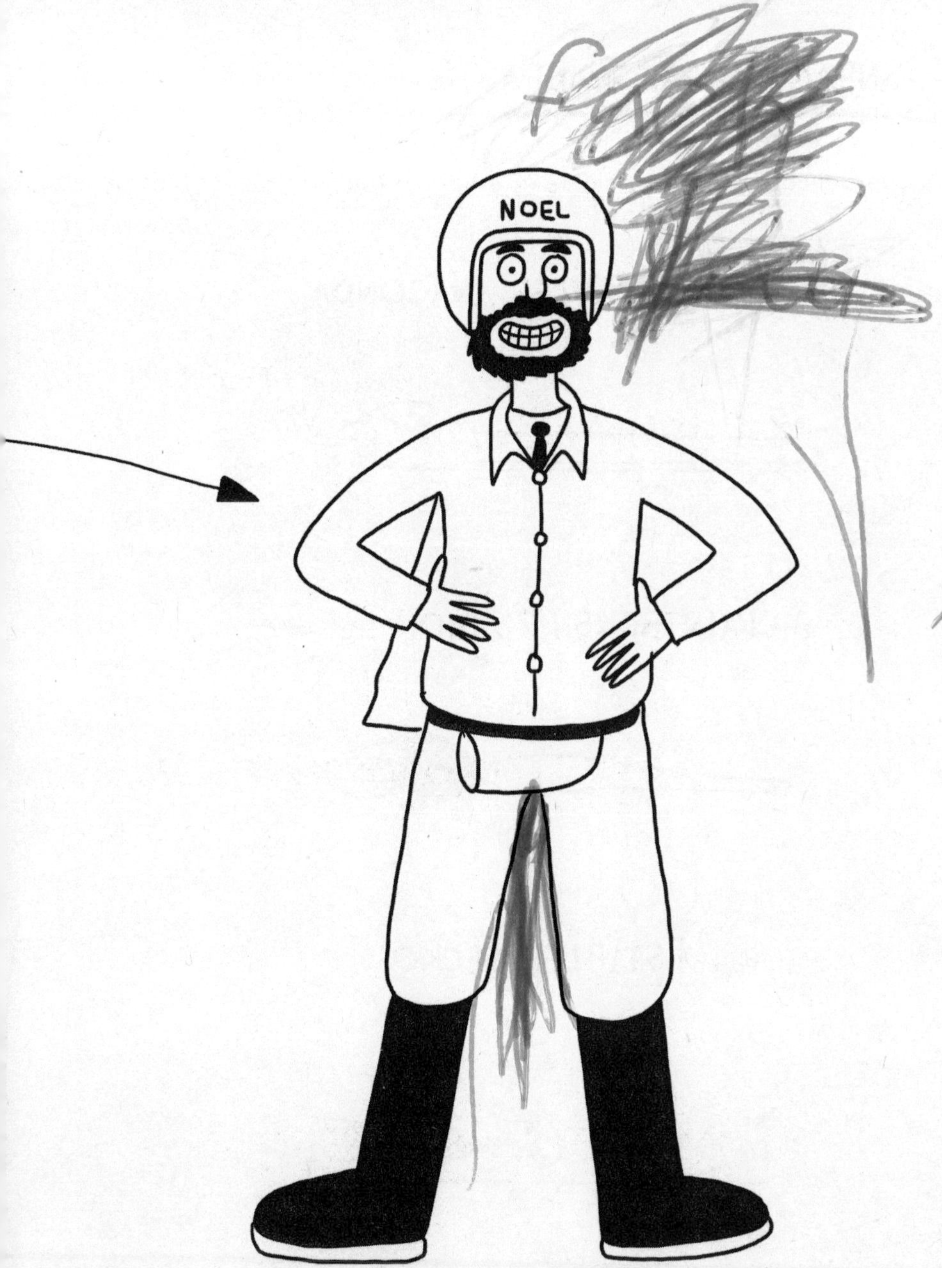
NOEL

3. SNEAKY SCHOOL BEASTS

Devious animals could be hiding in your school, waiting to chomp you.

Beware of the **RULER ANACONDA,**

the **PAINTBRUSH PYTHON,**

and the **STAPLER GECKO.**

4. THE SCHOOL LIBRARY

Not only home to the dreaded **PAGE NOEL SCORPION**, the school library can also be the location of **MANY OTHER AWFUL DANGERS**, such as:

BOOKVALANCHES (also known as **BOOKSHELF BARFS**)

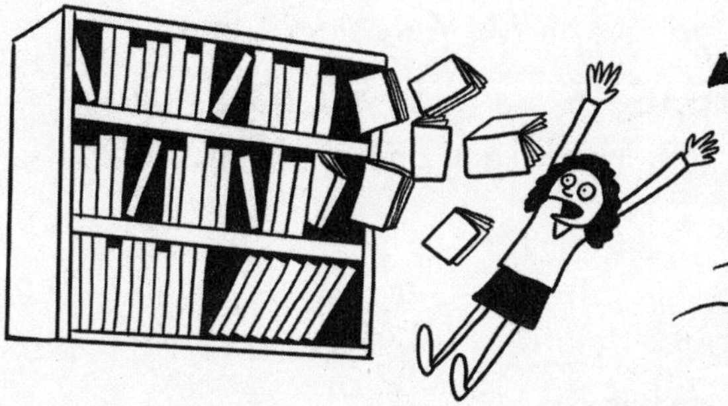

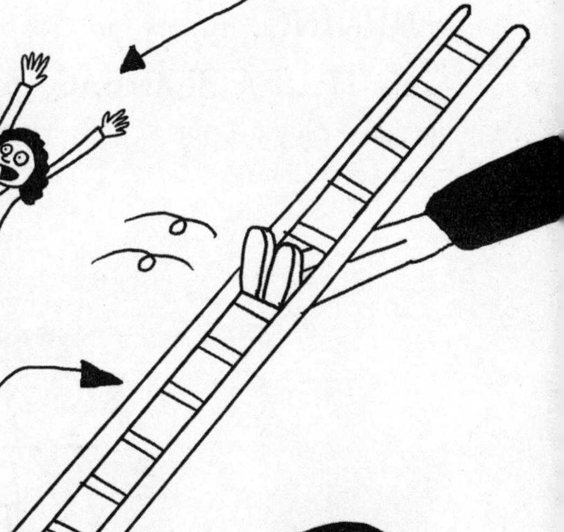

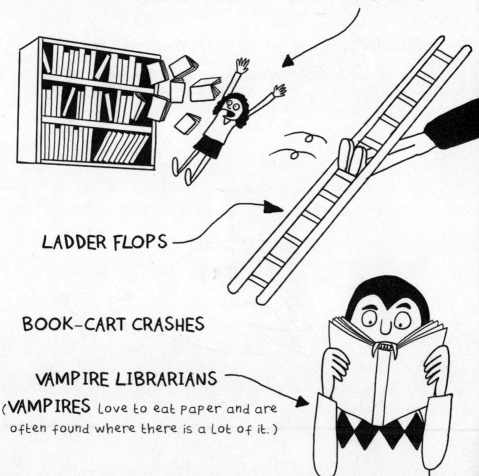

LADDER FLOPS

BOOK-CART CRASHES

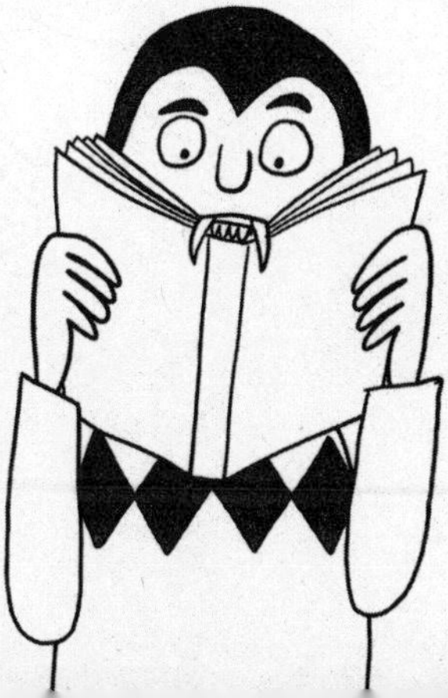

VAMPIRE LIBRARIANS
(**VAMPIRES** love to eat paper and are often found where there is a lot of it.)

5. SCHOOL CHAIRS

These are **MUCH** too dangerous, since daydreaming
students can easily topple off them. **ALL** chairs
should be replaced with **BEANBAGS**.

Desks are dangerous, too, and they should
be replaced with **BIGGER BEANBAGS**.

WARNING: Before you sit on **ANY** beanbag, make
sure **IT IS A BEANBAG** and not a **SEA LION** that has
wandered into your school by mistake and is trying
to take a nap.

6. NEW STUDENTS

Before welcoming any new students to school, make sure they **ARE DEFINITELY STUDENTS** and not **DANGEROUS ANIMALS IN DISGUISE** trying to sneak into your school **TO CHOMP EVERYONE.**

Some giveaways include:

-very large teeth or beaks

-saying their name is **GRRRRRR** or **RARR**

-eating their lunch with their face directly in the food while making this sound: **NOMF-NOMF-NOMF**

-having a big fin on their back and spending all their time in a big tank of water

7. SCHOOL BAGS

These are heavy and can hurt your back.

Much safer is a **BOOK-BARROW,**

a **COAT LIBRARY,**   or a **TEXTBOOK TAIL.**

CHAPTER ONE

SCHOOL!

It is Thursday morning and Daisy Doodle is on her way to school. It is a lovely sunny day. Or maybe it isn't because **THE WEATHER ISN'T DRAWN YET**.

Maybe the sun is shining or maybe there is a **HUGE** thunder and lightning storm. **YOU** decide, because that's the way this book works!

DRAW SOME WEATHER HERE.

So what's it going to be? Sunshine or rain? Daisy is hoping that it is sunny, because she has forgotten her coat.

Daisy arrives at school in a good mood. Or soaking wet. It really depends on what you drew.

She spots her best friend, Donny, outside the school gates. Donny gives her a big wave and runs over.

"Hey, Daisy. Did you see that movie about the alien invasion last night? It was cool!"

Daisy nods. "Yes, but why do they always make the aliens the bad guys? Some of them must be nice. I bet I could make friends with an alien if it came to visit Doodletown."

Donny laughs. "An alien in Doodletown? That's not going to happen, is it?"

"Well," says Daisy, "if I meet one, I'll let you know."

Daisy and Donny wander over to the playground. The bell hasn't rung yet so everyone is trying to have fun before school starts. Except they have forgotten to bring things to play with.

Look at these guys trying to jump without a jump rope. Can you draw one for them?

And these kids are playing soccer without a ball! Add one in with your pencil.

The bell rings, **DING-A-LING-A-LING!** It is time to line up for class. Miss Scribble comes out of the school to gather everyone together. But she seems to have forgotten something!

She waves her arms in front of her and stumbles around the playground. "Hello? Where is everybody?"

"It looks like she's lost her glasses again," says Daisy.
Can you draw some on her?

"Draw a **BIG MUSTACHE**, too!" says Donny.

Suddenly Miss Scribble can see.

"Ah, there you are," she says, twirling her
mustache. **TWIRLING HER MUSTACHE!?
WHAT THE—?**

"**EEEEK!** Who drew this mustache on me?" she
yells.

The whole class bursts out laughing. It's not every day
you see your teacher with a big handlebar mustache.

"That's enough fun for now," says Miss Scribble as she erases her mustache and straightens her glasses. "Everybody line up, please."

The whole class forms a line while Miss Scribble counts them. "Twenty-one, twenty-two. Twenty-two? We are one short. Where is Undrawn John?"

"I'm here," says a voice. "I'm just not drawn yet."

LOOK! IT'S UNDRAWN JOHN!

Miss Scribble sighs. "Can somebody please draw Undrawn John?"

Could you please help?

"Follow me," says Miss Scribble as she leads the class to the school entrance.

But look! Someone has erased the door while Miss Scribble wasn't looking.

"This is **RIDICULOUS**!" says Miss Scribble. "The door is gone again! Can anybody help?"

ENTRANCE

Quick! You had better draw a door before Daisy and her class get into more trouble.

Finally the school yard is empty. Which is too bad because the very next moment something **UNBELIEVABLE** happens.

AN ALIEN SPACESHIP FALLS FROM THE SKY!

Imagine! The one thing Daisy wanted to see and she just missed it by **ONE PAGE!**

The spaceship shoots across the sky, billowing smoke from its tail. Or at least it will be billowing smoke when you draw some billowing smoke.

DRAW LOTS OF SMOKE.

Exciting stuff, eh?

Meanwhile, inside, Miss Scribble is droning on about space and planets and stars. That might sound a bit **INTERESTING** to you, but Miss Scribble has a way of making the most **EXCITING** thing in the universe sound boring. Do you know any teachers like that?

No? Well, you are one of the lucky ones, I guess.

PLANET
SCRATCHPAD

SMILE
ISLAND

Miss Scribble is explaining that some planets are made out of rocks and some are made out of gas.

See what I mean? **EXCITING**. Not.

"Our Planet Scratchpad is just the right distance from the sun," she continues. "It is not too hot and not too cold. It is just the right temperature to allow us to live here. Like Goldilocks's porridge. Except it's not porridge. It's a planet. I hope you are taking notes."

Daisy is one of the few students still awake. "What sort of planets do aliens come from, Miss Scribble?"

Miss Scribble pauses mid-drone. "Daisy Doodle, how many times do I have to tell you? Aliens DON'T exist! Stop asking silly questions."

"Okay," says Daisy. "But what is that looking in the window then?"

Miss Scribble SCREAMS!

Because there is an **ALIEN** looking in the window!

DRAW A SCREAM!

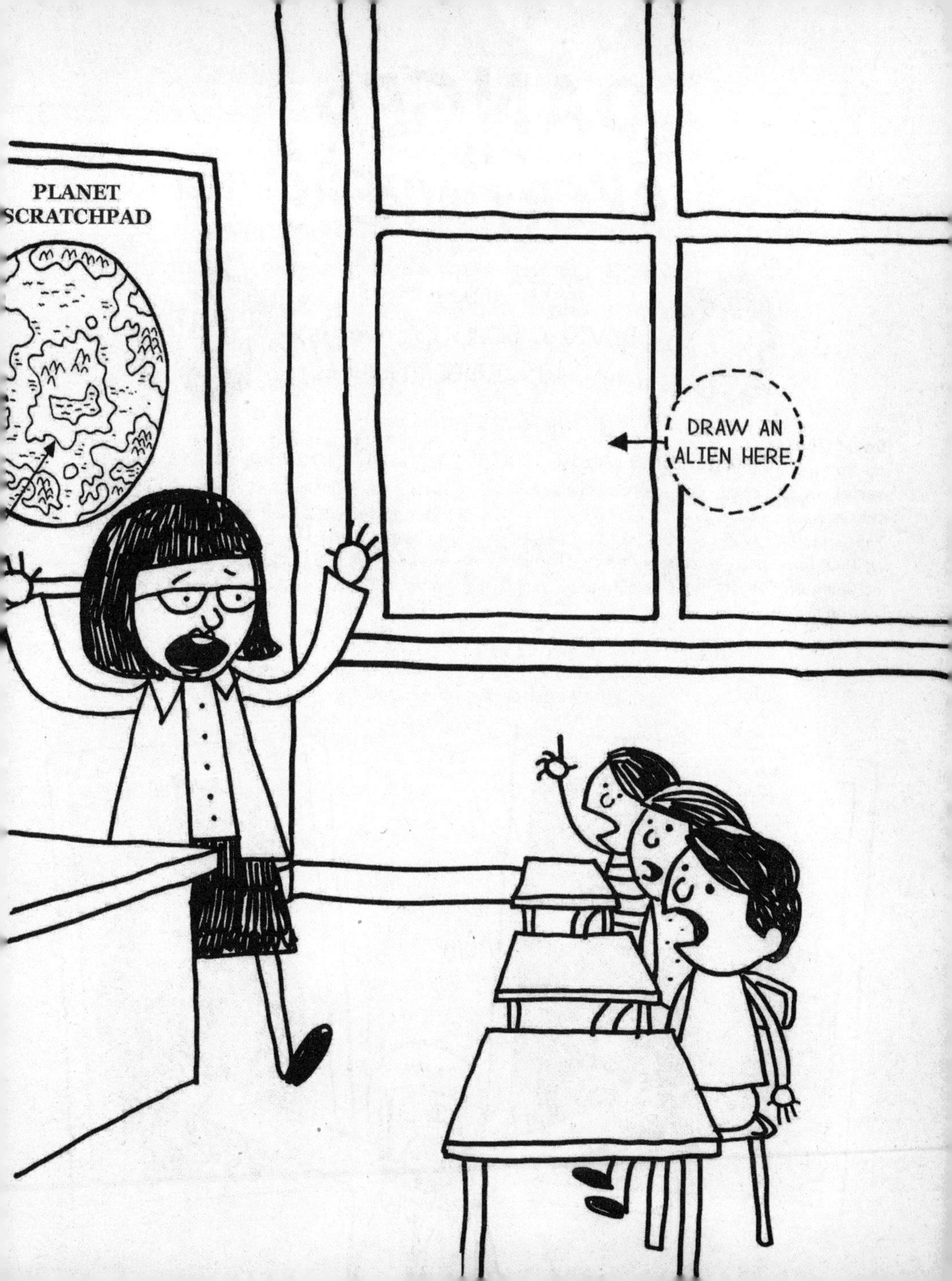
PLANET
SCRATCHPAD
DRAW AN
ALIEN HERE.

DANGER IS EVERYWHERE

was written with
the help of my neighbors

DAVID O'DOHERTY (words)
and CHRIS JUDGE (pictures)

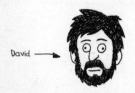

David →

← Chris

David O'Doherty is a comedian and the author of the Danger Is Everywhere series. He is a regular guest on television shows such as *QI, Have I Got News for You,* and *Would I Lie to You?,* and he has written two theater shows for children, including one where he fixed their bicycles live on stage.

Chris Judge is the illustrator of the Danger Is Everywhere series and the Draw-It-Yourself Adventures series. He is the award-winning author and illustrator of *The Lonely Beast* and a number of other picture books, and he most recently illustrated Roddy Doyle's novel *Brilliant.*

They met when Chris was in a band and David used to come and watch.
They both live in Dublin, Ireland.